ANNOYING ORANGE ™

HEY LOOK!

I'M ACTUAL SIZE!

PAPERCUT Z ™

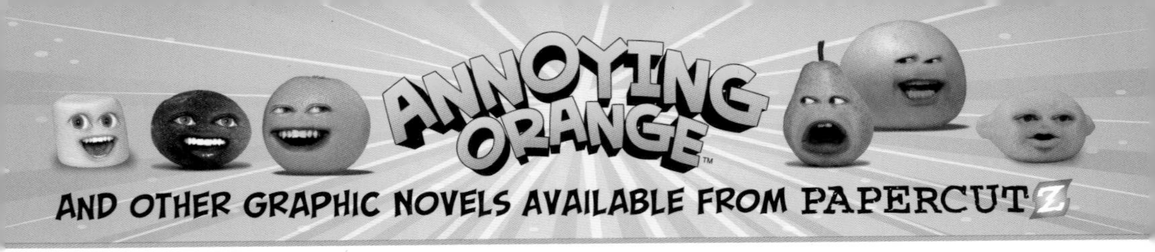
ANNOYING ORANGE
AND OTHER GRAPHIC NOVELS AVAILABLE FROM PAPERCUTZ

COMING SOON!

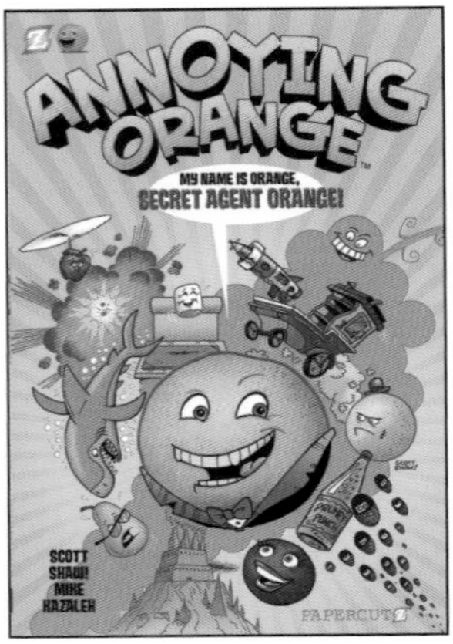
ANNOYING ORANGE
MY NAME IS ORANGE, SECRET AGENT ORANGE!
SCOTT SHAW! MIKE KAZALEH
PAPERCUTZ

ANNOYING ORANGE
Graphic Novel #1
"Secret Agent Orange"

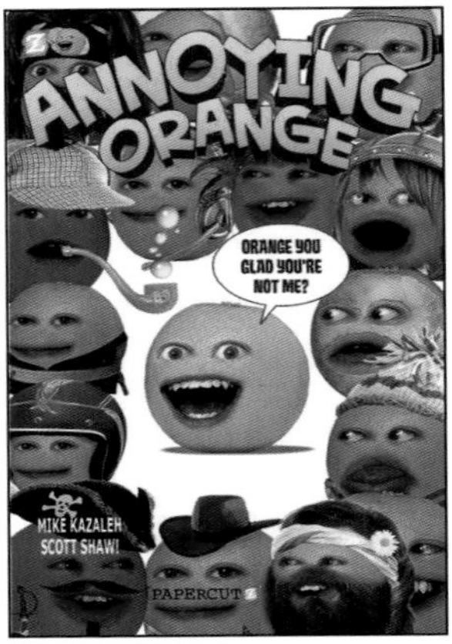
ANNOYING ORANGE
ORANGE YOU GLAD YOU'RE NOT ME?
MIKE KAZALEH SCOTT SHAW!
PAPERCUTZ

ANNOYING ORANGE
Graphic Novel #2
"Orange You Glad You're Not Me?"

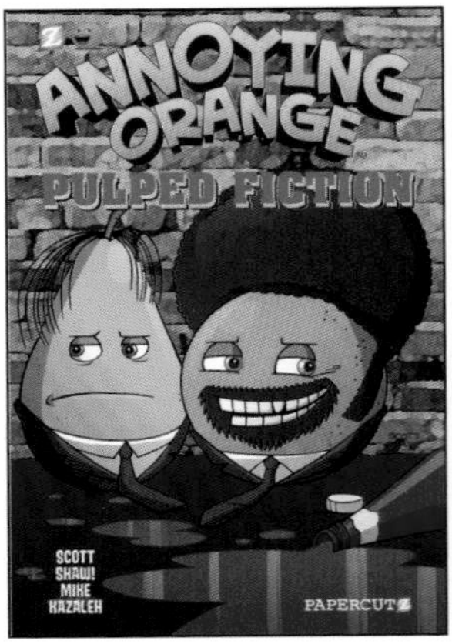
ANNOYING ORANGE
PULPED FICTION
SCOTT SHAW! MIKE KAZALEH
PAPERCUTZ

ANNOYING ORANGE
Graphic Novel #3
"Pulped Fiction"

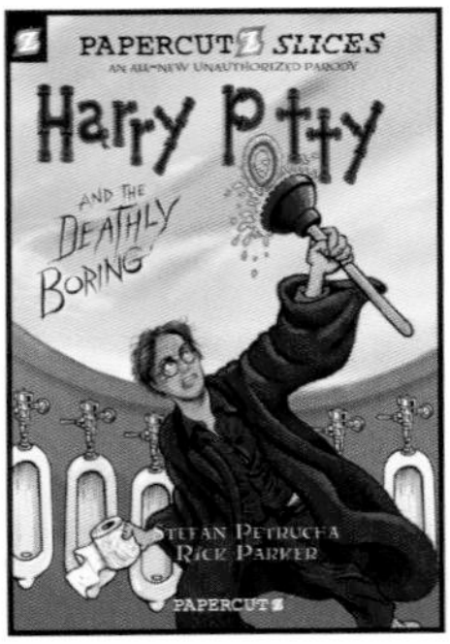
PAPERCUTZ SLICES
Harry Potty
AND THE DEATHLY BORING
STEFAN PETRUCHA RICK PARKER
PAPERCUTZ

PAPERCUTZ SLICES
Graphic Novel #1
"Harry Potty and the Deathly Boring"

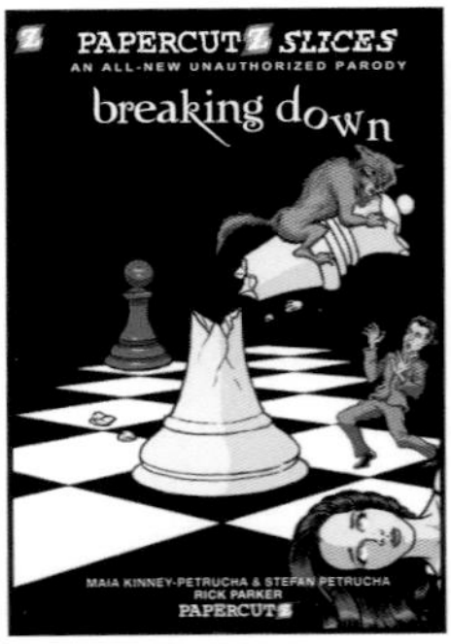
PAPERCUTZ SLICES
AN ALL-NEW UNAUTHORIZED PARODY
breaking down
MAIA KINNEY-PETRUCHA & STEFAN PETRUCHA
RICK PARKER
PAPERCUTZ

PAPERCUTZ SLICES
Graphic Novel #2
"breaking down"

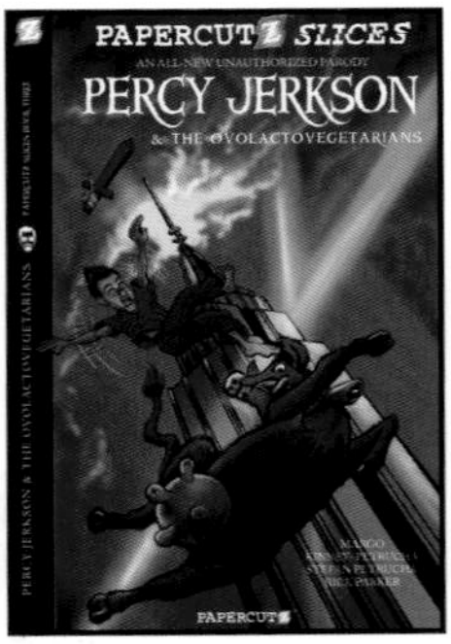
PAPERCUTZ SLICES
AN ALL-NEW UNAUTHORIZED PARODY
PERCY JERKSON
& THE OVOLACTOVEGETARIANS
PAPERCUTZ

PAPERCUTZ SLICES
Graphic Novel #3
"Percy Jerkson & The Ovolactovegetarians"

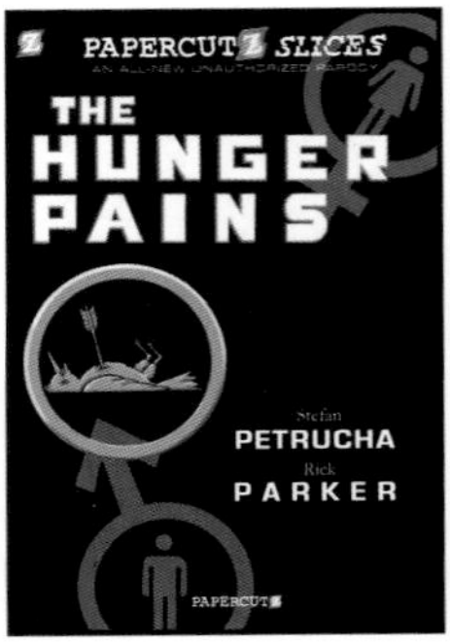
PAPERCUTZ SLICES
THE HUNGER PAINS
Stefan PETRUCHA
Rick PARKER
PAPERCUTZ

PAPERCUTZ SLICES
Graphic Novel #4
"The Hunger Pains"

ANNOYING ORANGE and PAPERCUTZ SLICES graphic novels, the print editions, are still available at booksellers everywhere.

Or order directly from Papercutz. ANNOYING ORANGE and PAPERCUTZ SLICES are available in paperback for $6.99 each; in hardcover for $10.99, except ANNOYING ORANGE #2, hardcover is $11.99, and ANNOYING ORANGE #3 is $7.99 paperback, and $11.99 hardcover. Please add $4.00 for postage and handling for the first book, and add $1.00 for each additional book. Make check payable to NBM Publishing.

Send to: Papercutz, 160 Broadway, Suite 700, East Wing, New York, NY 10038

Or call 800-886-1223 between 9-5 EST, M-F. Visa, MC, and AmEx accepted.

www.papercutz.com

ANNOYING ORANGE and PAPERCUTZ SLICES graphic novels are also available digitally wherever e-books are sold.

ORANGE YOU GLAD YOU'RE NOT ME?

WHY HIM, AND NOT ME?! THIS SHOULD BE MY GRAPHIC NOVEL!

Annoying Orange is created by DANE BOEDIGHEIMER

SCOTT SHAW! – Writer & Artist

MIKE KAZALEH – Writer & Artist

LAURIE E. SMITH – Colorist

PAPERCUTZ

NEW YORK

ANNOYING ORANGE™

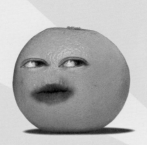

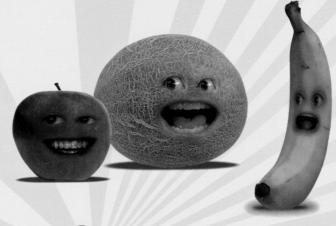

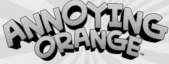

2 "Orange You Glad You're Not Me?"

"There's No Business as Annoying as Show Business!"
"Part of This Ridiculous Breakfast!"
"What's the Skinny on Mr. Fat-Citrus?"
"A Date is Not Just a Dried Fruit!"
"The Quest for the Golden Grail!"
"Not Everything He's Cracked Up to Be!"
Scott Shaw! – Writer & Artist
Laurie E. Smith – Colorist
Tom Orzechowski – Letterer
"Orange You Glad You're Not Me?"
Mike Kazaleh – Writer & Artist
Laurie E. Smith – Colorist
Tom Orzechowski – Letterer

Special thanks to: Gary Binkow, Tim Blankley, Dane Boedigheimer, Kristy Fagan, Spencer Grove, Teresa Harris, Reza Izad, Debra Joester, Polina Rey, Tom Sheppard
Design & Production: Nelson Design Group, LLC
Director of Marketing: Jesse Post
Production Coordinator: Beth Scorzato
Associate Editor: Michael Petranek
Jim Salicrup
Editor-in-Chief

ISBN: 978-1-59707-390-5 paperback edition
ISBN: 978-1-59707-391-2 hardcover edition

Printed in Canada
May 2013 by Friesens Printing
1 Printers Way
Altona, MB ROG OBO

Papercutz books may be purchased for business or promotional use.
For information on bulk purchases please contact Macmillan Corporate and Premium Sales Department at (800) 221-7945 x5442.

Distributed by Macmillan
First Printing

MEET THE FRUIT...

HERE'S A GUY WITH A LOT OF *APPEAL*...

YEAH! *ORANGE PEEL!* HA! HA! HA!

ORANGE

Since the debut of ANNOYING ORANGE #1 "Secret Agent Orange," the Orange-loving public has wondered on Internet Bulletin Boards and on school bathroom walls exactly how the world-famous fruity cast of the hit Cartoon Network TV series has been turned into graphic novel characters. Well, it turns out it wasn't all that difficult! Today's award-winning graphic novels tend to feature characters who have lead extraordinary lives. Harvey and Eisner Award Committees please take note—here at last is the powerful tale of a young orange who has dared to be... annoying!

PEAR

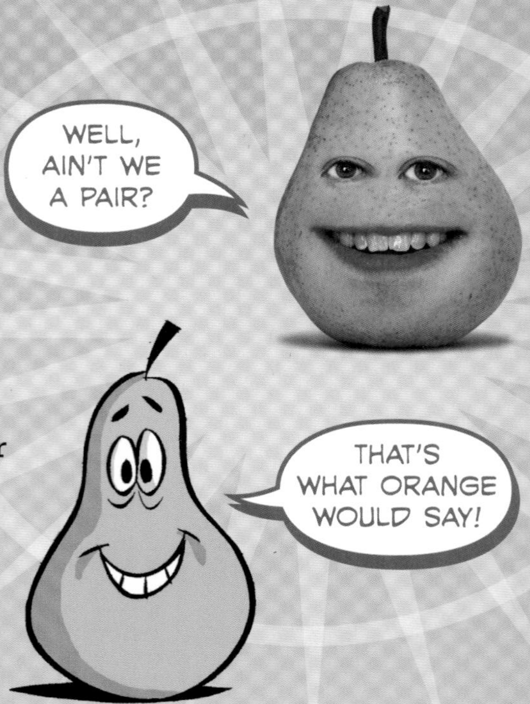
WELL, AIN'T WE A PAIR?
THAT'S WHAT ORANGE WOULD SAY!

In keeping with a literary tradition that has included Steinbeck's Lenny and George and Marshall's Lenny and Squiggy, Pear is the character that Orange considers his best friend. That is if he were to consider such things. Pear spent considerable time posing for graphic novel artists Scott Shaw! and Mike Kazaleh in order to achieve a perfect likeness, and upon seeing the artistic results, Pear opined "whatever."

MIDGET APPLE

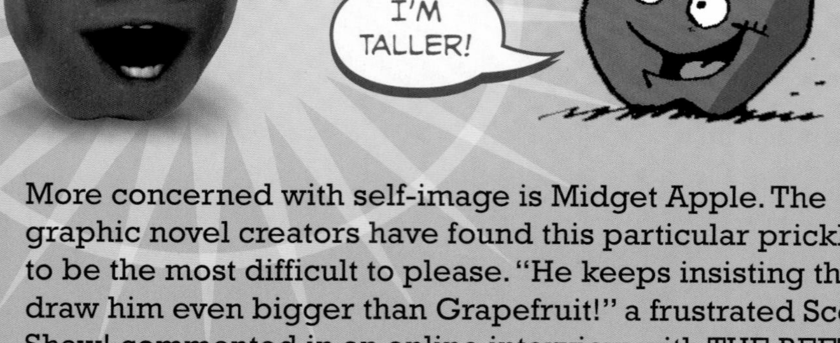
THAT'S *LITTLE* APPLE!
I'M TALLER!

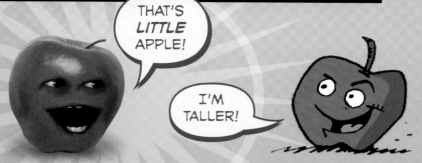

More concerned with self-image is Midget Apple. The graphic novel creators have found this particular prickly fruit to be the most difficult to please. "He keeps insisting that we draw him even bigger than Grapefruit!" a frustrated Scott Shaw! commented in an online interview with THE BEET's Heidi Macintosh. "But in the interests of journalistic truth—and because our editor told us to ignore Midget Apple—we're drawing him just as we see him. Small. Very Small."

PASSION FRUIT

I'M SIMPLY BESIDE MYSELF!

Such a potentially award-winning graphic novel saga must also focus on the characters who populate our hero's world—in this case the produce section of Daneboe's Supermarket. Making the transition from the computer screen to the TV screen and now onto the printed page (and then back on the computer screen in the digital edition!) Passion Fruit is once again cast in the role of the loyal, supportive female who clearly has affection for Orange despite his tendency to be… annoying. Yes, the women do like their bad boys!

MARSHMALLOW

I LOVE BEING ME!

ME TOO! YAY!

Perhaps there's no character in this amazing saga more mystifying than Marshmallow. Marshmallow is virtually the living embodiment of pure positivity despite being so out of place! Critics love such enigmatic characters and we love Marshmallow! Yay!

GRANDPA LEMON

Just as "Maus," the famed graphic novel by Pulitzer Prize-winning cartoonist Art Spiegelman, featured a dialogue between father and son, Grandpa Lemon is the voice of an earlier generation. In the already classic "The Salad Days of Grandpa Lemon," from ANNOYING ORANGE #1 "Secret Agent Orange," not only was the story particularly poignant, Grandpa Lemon made the brave choice to play his role wearing his never-before-seen glasses. A controversial decision that got him in hot water with the TV show's producers. But lemons are used to being in hot water, so it was no big deal.

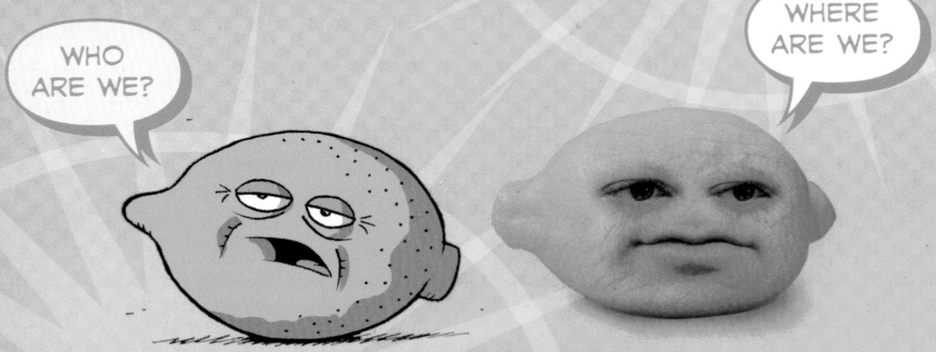
WHO ARE WE?
WHERE ARE WE?

GRAPEFRUIT

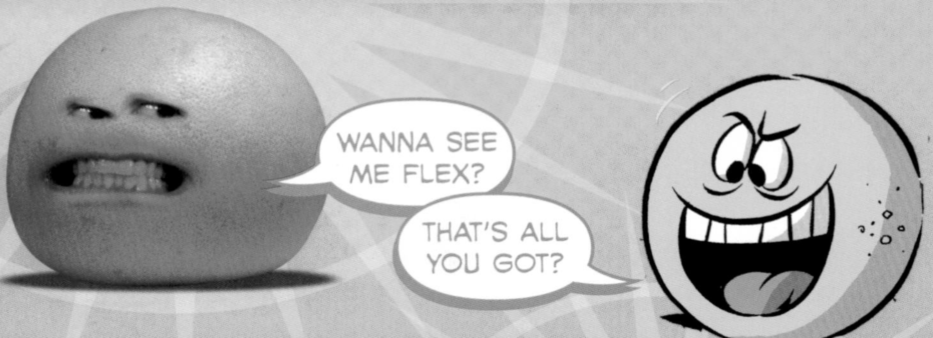
WANNA SEE ME FLEX?
THAT'S ALL YOU GOT?

Grapefruit, convinced he's being held back by the limitations of the small screen, is convinced that he may actually thrive in the graphic novel format. Comparing himself to such classic comics characters as "The Incredible Hulk" and "Stumbo," Grapefruit believes comics may be an ideal showcase for his massive muscular macho persona. At press time, it seems the jury is still out on that one, but who knows?

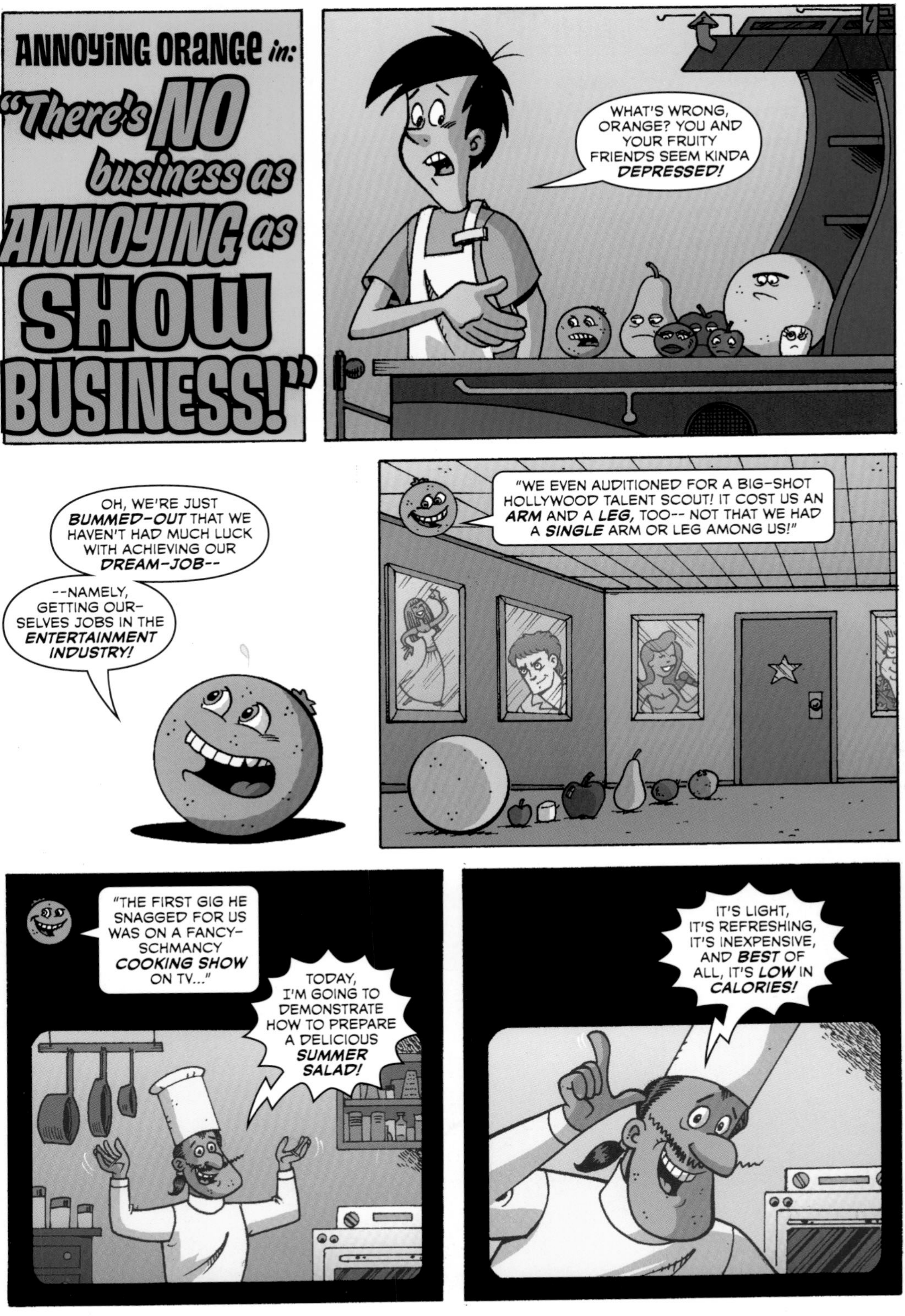
ANNOYING ORANGE in:
"There's NO business as ANNOYING as SHOW BUSINESS!"
WHAT'S WRONG, ORANGE? YOU AND YOUR FRUITY FRIENDS SEEM KINDA DEPRESSED!
OH, WE'RE JUST BUMMED-OUT THAT WE HAVEN'T HAD MUCH LUCK WITH ACHIEVING OUR DREAM-JOB--
--NAMELY, GETTING OUR-SELVES JOBS IN THE ENTERTAINMENT INDUSTRY!
"WE EVEN AUDITIONED FOR A BIG-SHOT HOLLYWOOD TALENT SCOUT! IT COST US AN ARM AND A LEG, TOO-- NOT THAT WE HAD A SINGLE ARM OR LEG AMONG US!"
"THE FIRST GIG HE SNAGGED FOR US WAS ON A FANCY-SCHMANCY COOKING SHOW ON TV..."
TODAY, I'M GOING TO DEMONSTRATE HOW TO PREPARE A DELICIOUS SUMMER SALAD!
IT'S LIGHT, IT'S REFRESHING, IT'S INEXPENSIVE, AND BEST OF ALL, IT'S LOW IN CALORIES!

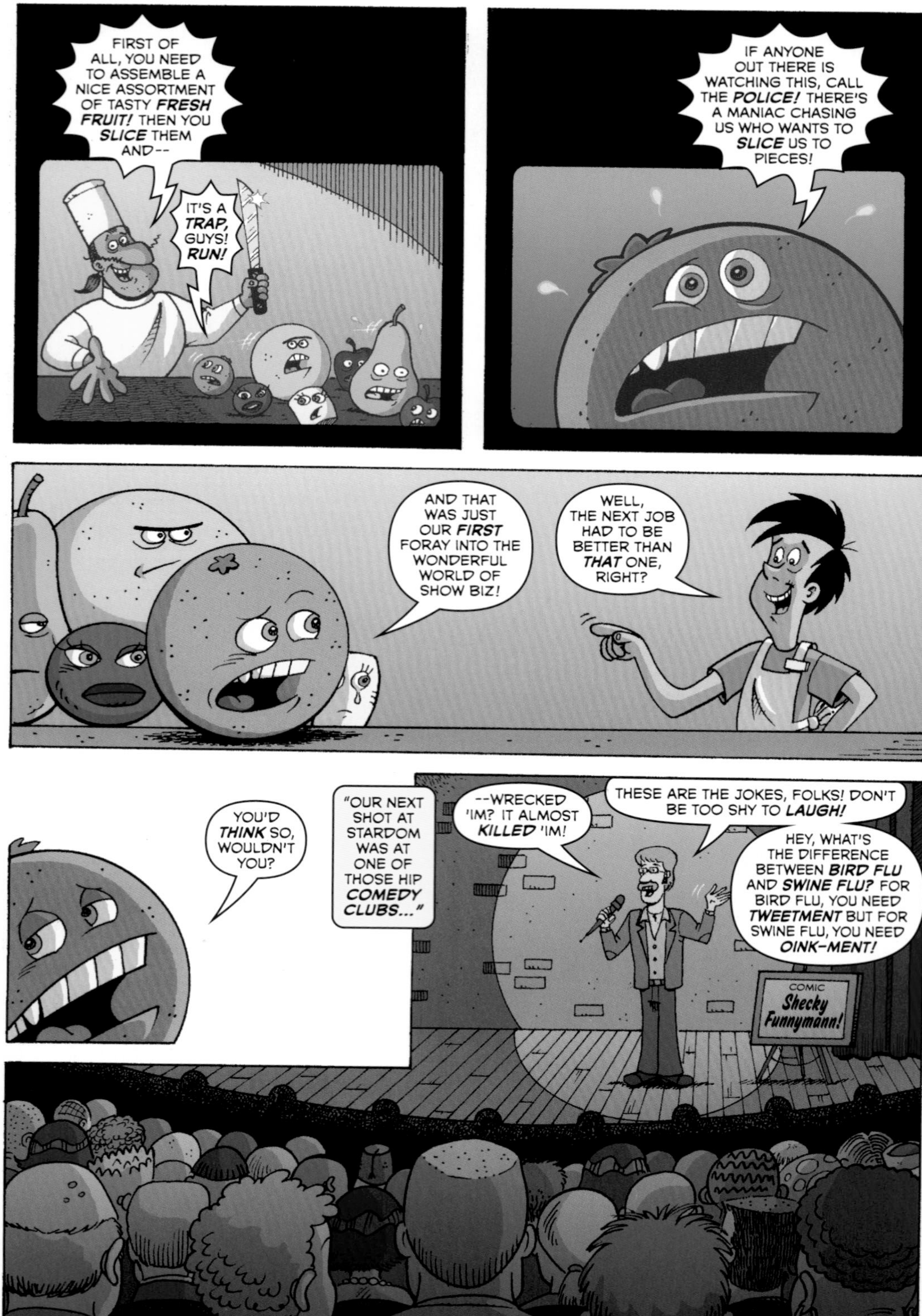
FIRST OF ALL, YOU NEED TO ASSEMBLE A NICE ASSORTMENT OF TASTY FRESH FRUIT! THEN YOU SLICE THEM AND--
IT'S A TRAP, GUYS! RUN!
IF ANYONE OUT THERE IS WATCHING THIS, CALL THE POLICE! THERE'S A MANIAC CHASING US WHO WANTS TO SLICE US TO PIECES!
AND THAT WAS JUST OUR FIRST FORAY INTO THE WONDERFUL WORLD OF SHOW BIZ!
WELL, THE NEXT JOB HAD TO BE BETTER THAN THAT ONE, RIGHT?
YOU'D THINK SO, WOULDN'T YOU?
"OUR NEXT SHOT AT STARDOM WAS AT ONE OF THOSE HIP COMEDY CLUBS..."
--WRECKED 'IM? IT ALMOST KILLED 'IM!
THESE ARE THE JOKES, FOLKS! DON'T BE TOO SHY TO LAUGH!
HEY, WHAT'S THE DIFFERENCE BETWEEN BIRD FLU AND SWINE FLU? FOR BIRD FLU, YOU NEED TWEETMENT BUT FOR SWINE FLU, YOU NEED OINK-MENT!
COMIC Shecky Funnymann!

HOWZAT? FUNNY STUFF, HUH?

=GROAN!=

=SIGH!=

=YECCH!=

=FEH!=

UH-OH!

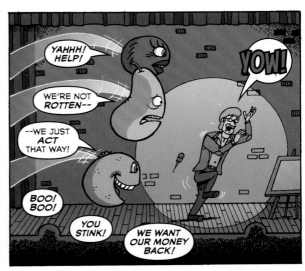

YAHHH! HELP!

YOW!

WE'RE NOT ROTTEN--

--WE JUST ACT THAT WAY!

BOO! BOO!

YOU STINK!

WE WANT OUR MONEY BACK!

OMIGOSH! WERE YOU GUYS HURT?

NAH, WE JUST GOT A FEW BRUISES AND I SCRAPED MY RIND!

"THEN, WE GOT BOOKED ON A TV GAME SHOW! AT FIRST, IT SEEMED LIKE IT'D BE EASY, BUT THEN..."

the BIG PAYOFF!

WELCOME TO BIG BUCK$, THE GAME SHOW WHERE EVEN AN IDIOT CAN BECOME A ZILLIONAIRE-- JUST BY PULLING A LEVER!

RIGHT, CHUCK!

OOH! AHH! WOW!

AND THIS IDIOT JUST CAN'T WAIT TO PLAY! =UMPH!=

YANK

"AND THAT'S WHEN IT ALL WENT BAD... REAL BAD!"

AHHH! WHOAAA! =BLECHHH!=

TWIRL

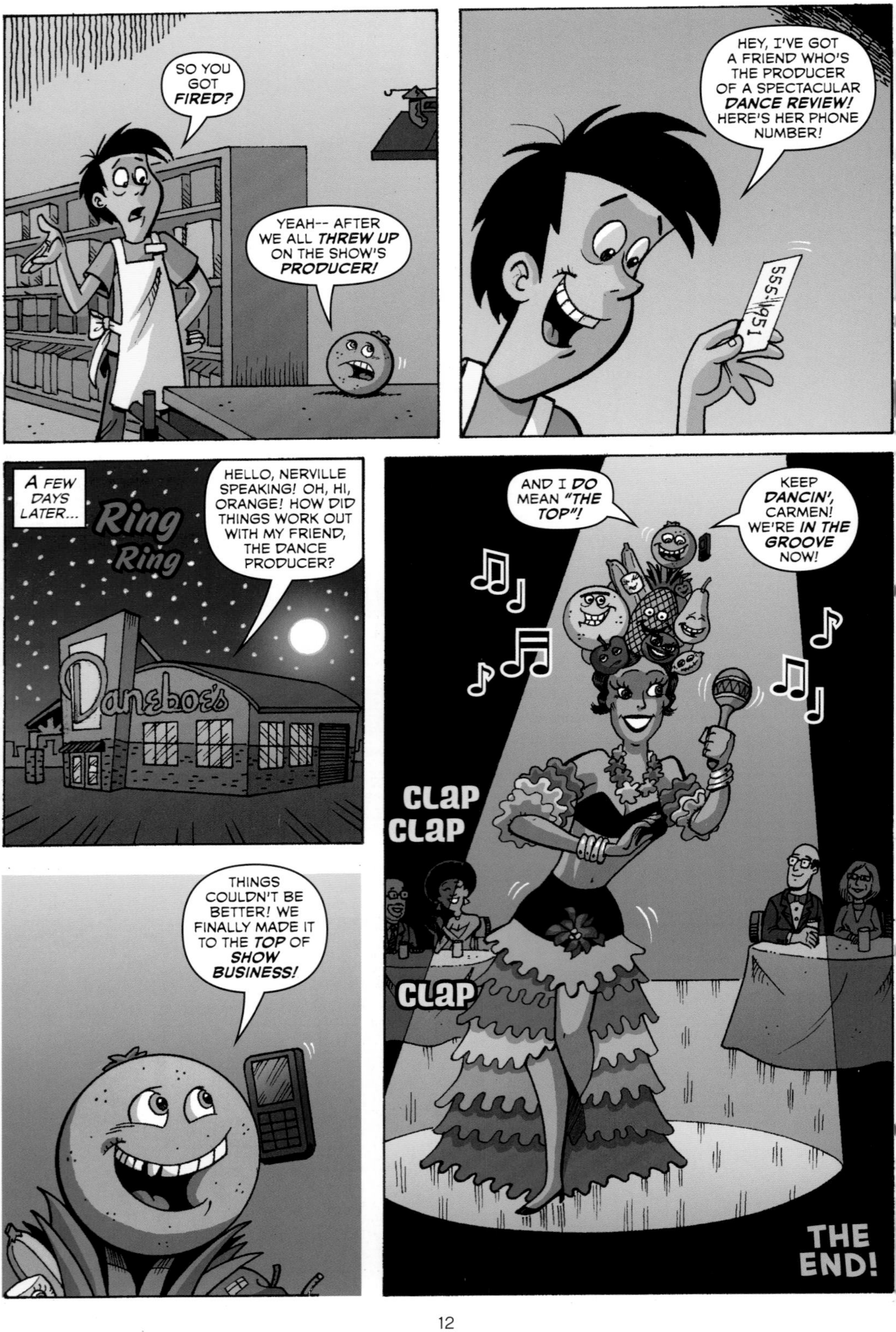
SO YOU GOT FIRED?
YEAH-- AFTER WE ALL THREW UP ON THE SHOW'S PRODUCER!
HEY, I'VE GOT A FRIEND WHO'S THE PRODUCER OF A SPECTACULAR DANCE REVIEW! HERE'S HER PHONE NUMBER!
555-1951
A FEW DAYS LATER...
Ring Ring
HELLO, NERVILLE SPEAKING! OH, HI, ORANGE! HOW DID THINGS WORK OUT WITH MY FRIEND, THE DANCE PRODUCER?
Dansboe's
THINGS COULDN'T BE BETTER! WE FINALLY MADE IT TO THE TOP OF SHOW BUSINESS!
AND I DO MEAN "THE TOP"!
KEEP DANCIN', CARMEN! WE'RE IN THE GROOVE NOW!
CLAP CLAP
CLAP
THE END!

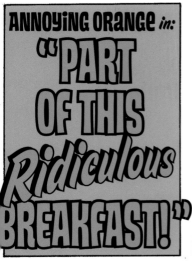

ANNOYING ORANGE *in:*

"PART OF THIS *Ridiculous* BREAKFAST!"

WOW, I ACTUALLY GOT SOME *MAIL!* MAYBE IT'S FROM A BEAUTIFUL *FAN-FRUIT!*

HMMM, IT'S FROM A BIG-TIME *CEREAL MANUFACTURER!*

"DEAR MR. ORANGE..."

WHAT'S *UP,* ORANGE?

THIS IS WHAT'S UP-- SO *READ IT!* I'LL EVEN HELP YOU WITH THE *BIG WORDS!*

"DEAR MR. ORANGE, I REPRESENT THE MILLSTONE CEREAL CO. WE WANT YOU AND YOUR FRIENDS TO APPEAR ON OUR *FRUITY POLYHEDRONS* CEREAL BOXES AND TV COMMERCIALS."

"WE LOOK FORWARD TO A LONG AND EXTREMELY PROFITABLE RELATIONSHIP." WOW, THESE GUYS ARE *SERIOUS,* ORANGE!

I ESPECIALLY DIG THAT *"EXTREMELY PROFITABLE"* PART! SO, *WHAT* IS A *"POLYHEDRON,"* ANYWAY?

SOON, NERVILLE AND HIS FRUITY FRIENDS GO ONLINE TO LEARN MORE ABOUT THE CEREAL COMPANY...

HERE IT IS, GANG-- A TV COMMERCIAL FOR MILLSTONE'S *FRUITY POLYHEDRONS* CEREAL!

WELL, WHY WASTE TIME? *CLICK ON* THAT BAD BOY!

CLICK

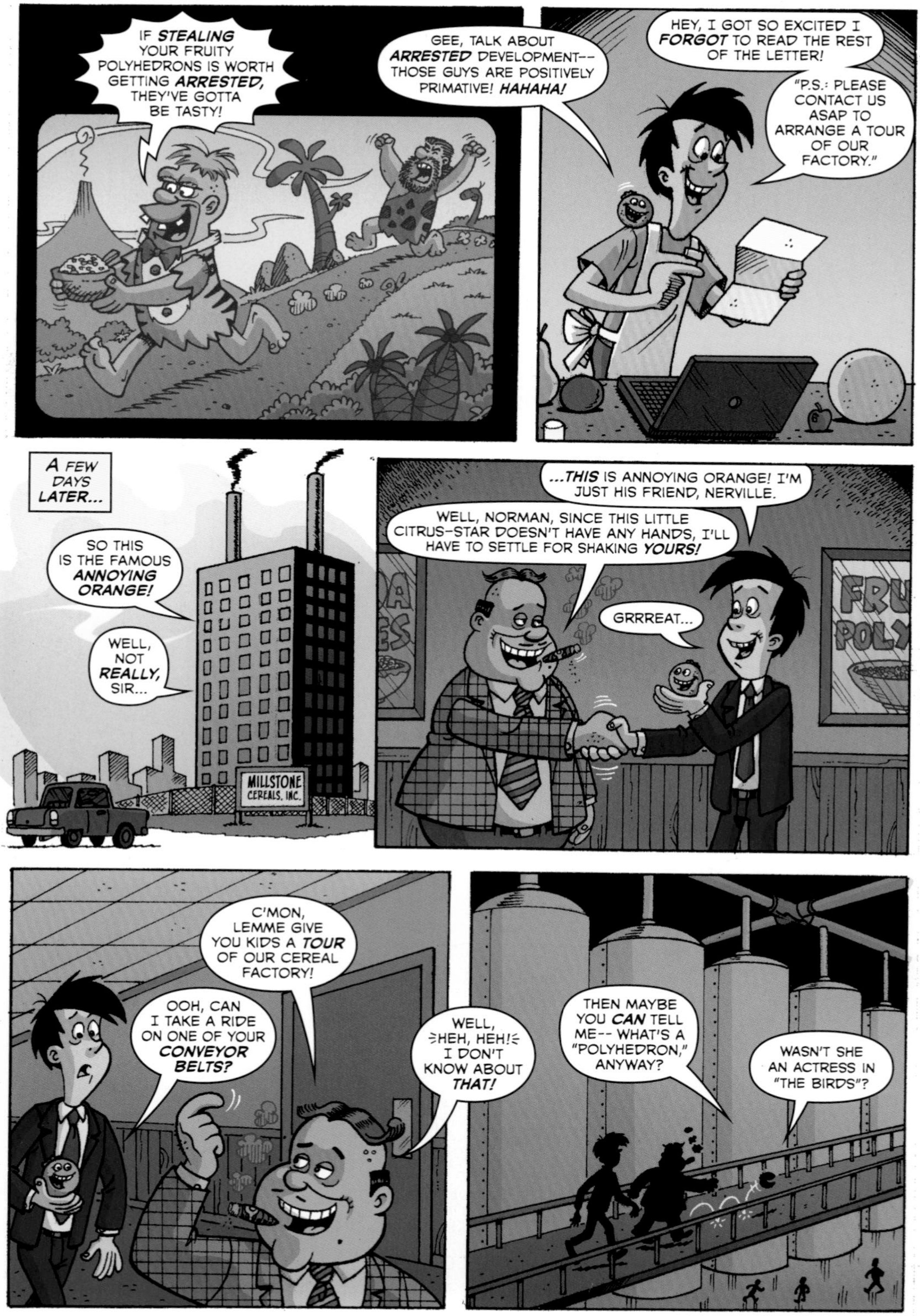
IF STEALING YOUR FRUITY POLYHEDRONS IS WORTH GETTING ARRESTED, THEY'VE GOTTA BE TASTY!
GEE, TALK ABOUT ARRESTED DEVELOPMENT-- THOSE GUYS ARE POSITIVELY PRIMATIVE! HAHAHA!
HEY, I GOT SO EXCITED I FORGOT TO READ THE REST OF THE LETTER!
"P.S.: PLEASE CONTACT US ASAP TO ARRANGE A TOUR OF OUR FACTORY."
A FEW DAYS LATER...
SO THIS IS THE FAMOUS ANNOYING ORANGE!
WELL, NOT REALLY, SIR...
MILLSTONE CEREALS, INC.
...THIS IS ANNOYING ORANGE! I'M JUST HIS FRIEND, NERVILLE.
WELL, NORMAN, SINCE THIS LITTLE CITRUS-STAR DOESN'T HAVE ANY HANDS, I'LL HAVE TO SETTLE FOR SHAKING YOURS!
GRRREAT...
C'MON, LEMME GIVE YOU KIDS A TOUR OF OUR CEREAL FACTORY!
OOH, CAN I TAKE A RIDE ON ONE OF YOUR CONVEYOR BELTS?
WELL, HEH, HEH! I DON'T KNOW ABOUT THAT!
THEN MAYBE YOU CAN TELL ME-- WHAT'S A "POLYHEDRON," ANYWAY?
WASN'T SHE AN ACTRESS IN "THE BIRDS"?

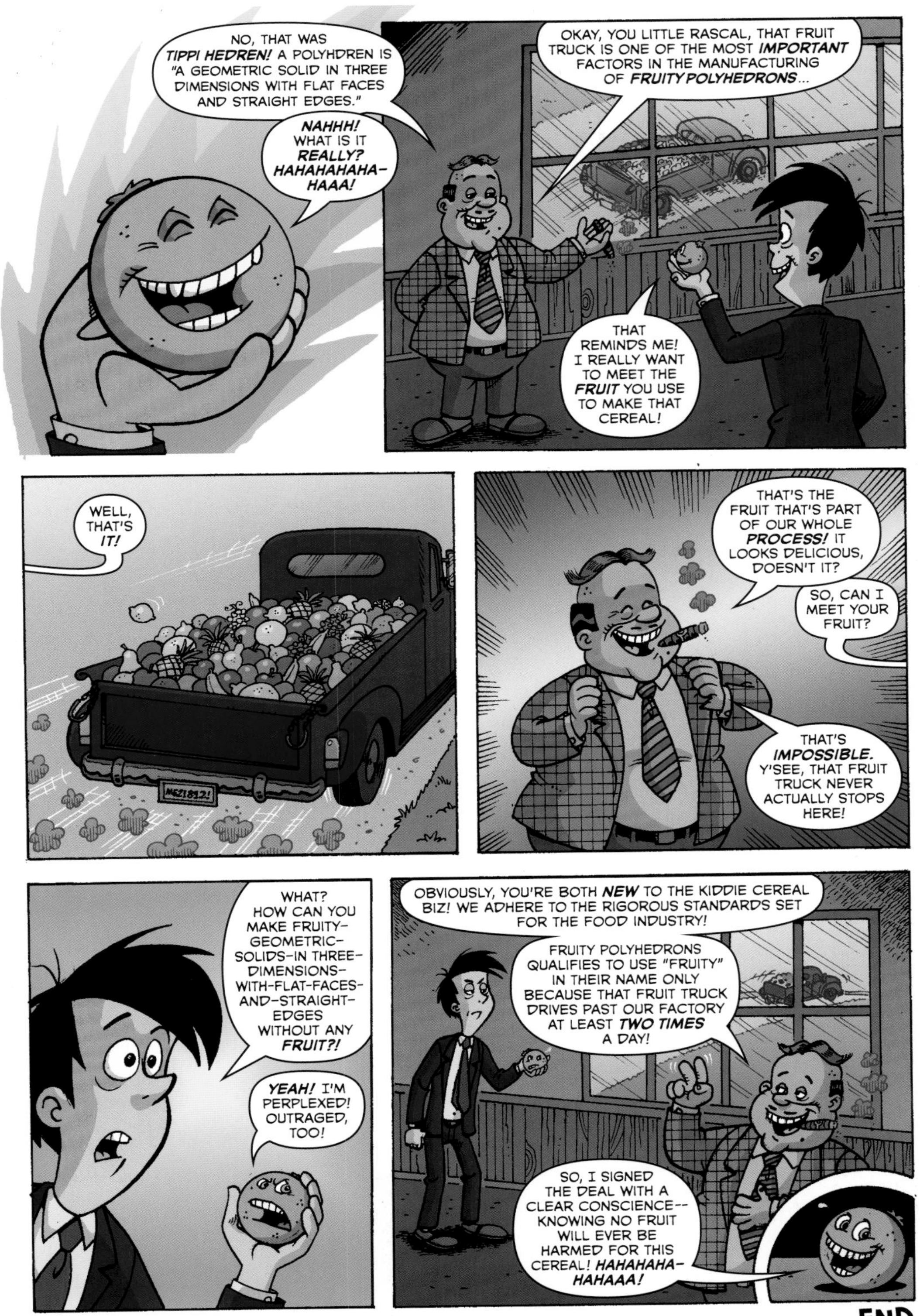
NO, THAT WAS TIPPI HEDREN! A POLYHDREN IS "A GEOMETRIC SOLID IN THREE DIMENSIONS WITH FLAT FACES AND STRAIGHT EDGES."
NAHHH! WHAT IS IT REALLY? HAHAHAHAHA-HAAA!
OKAY, YOU LITTLE RASCAL, THAT FRUIT TRUCK IS ONE OF THE MOST IMPORTANT FACTORS IN THE MANUFACTURING OF FRUITY POLYHEDRONS...
THAT REMINDS ME! I REALLY WANT TO MEET THE FRUIT YOU USE TO MAKE THAT CEREAL!
WELL, THAT'S IT!
THAT'S THE FRUIT THAT'S PART OF OUR WHOLE PROCESS! IT LOOKS DELICIOUS, DOESN'T IT?
SO, CAN I MEET YOUR FRUIT?
THAT'S IMPOSSIBLE. Y'SEE, THAT FRUIT TRUCK NEVER ACTUALLY STOPS HERE!
WHAT? HOW CAN YOU MAKE FRUITY-GEOMETRIC-SOLIDS-IN THREE-DIMENSIONS-WITH-FLAT-FACES-AND-STRAIGHT-EDGES WITHOUT ANY FRUIT?!
YEAH! I'M PERPLEXED! OUTRAGED, TOO!
OBVIOUSLY, YOU'RE BOTH NEW TO THE KIDDIE CEREAL BIZ! WE ADHERE TO THE RIGOROUS STANDARDS SET FOR THE FOOD INDUSTRY!
FRUITY POLYHEDRONS QUALIFIES TO USE "FRUITY" IN THEIR NAME ONLY BECAUSE THAT FRUIT TRUCK DRIVES PAST OUR FACTORY AT LEAST TWO TIMES A DAY!
SO, I SIGNED THE DEAL WITH A CLEAR CONSCIENCE-- KNOWING NO FRUIT WILL EVER BE HARMED FOR THIS CEREAL! HAHAHAHA-HAHAAA!
END

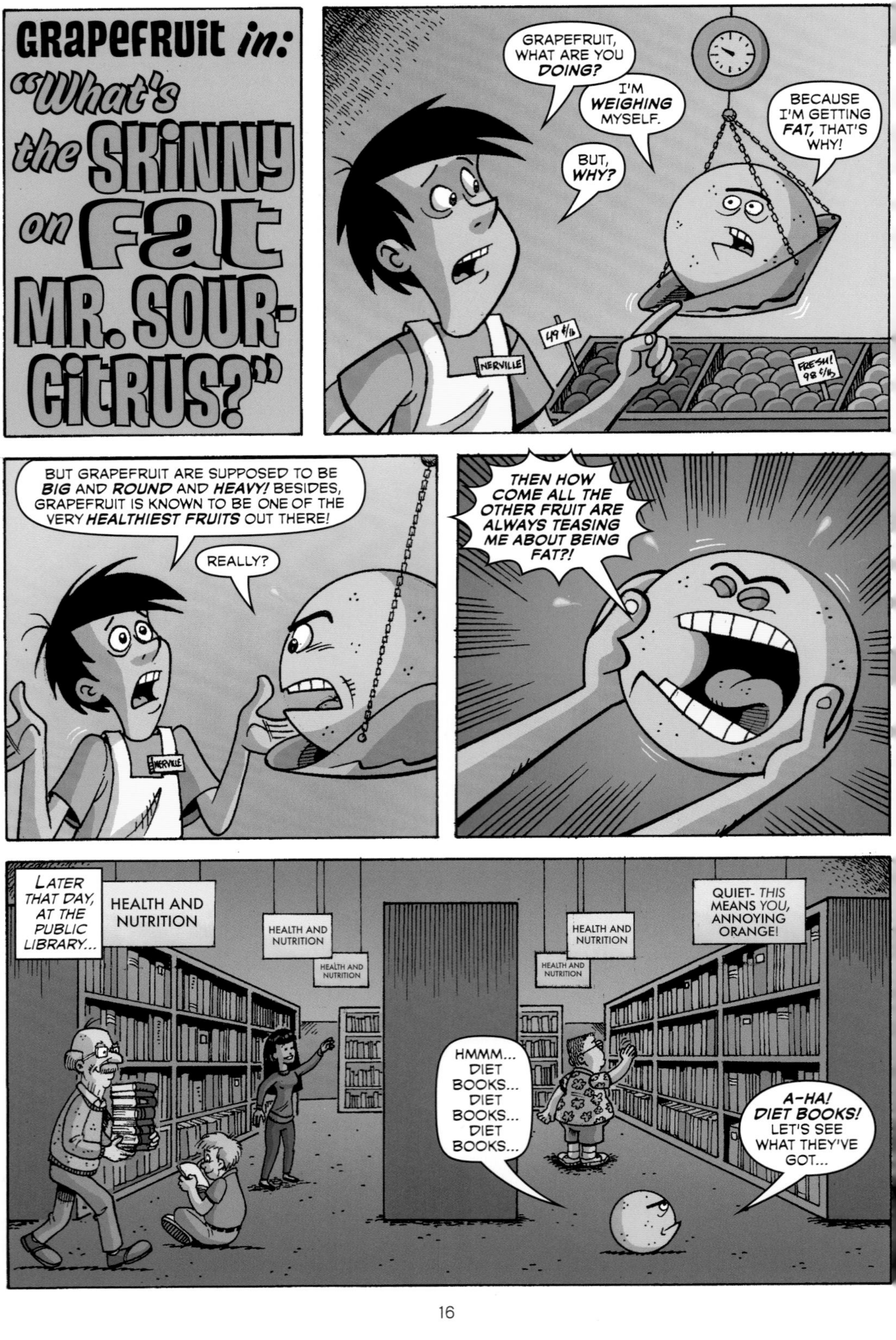

GRAPEFRUIT in: "What's the SKINNY on FAT MR. SOUR-CITRUS?"
GRAPEFRUIT, WHAT ARE YOU DOING?
I'M WEIGHING MYSELF.
BUT, WHY?
BECAUSE I'M GETTING FAT, THAT'S WHY!
49 ¢/lb
NERVILLE
FRESH! 98 ¢/lb
BUT GRAPEFRUIT ARE SUPPOSED TO BE BIG AND ROUND AND HEAVY! BESIDES, GRAPEFRUIT IS KNOWN TO BE ONE OF THE VERY HEALTHIEST FRUITS OUT THERE!
REALLY?
NERVILLE
THEN HOW COME ALL THE OTHER FRUIT ARE ALWAYS TEASING ME ABOUT BEING FAT?!
LATER THAT DAY, AT THE PUBLIC LIBRARY...
HEALTH AND NUTRITION
HEALTH AND NUTRITION
HEALTH AND NUTRITION
HEALTH AND NUTRITION
HEALTH AND NUTRITION
QUIET- THIS MEANS YOU, ANNOYING ORANGE!
HMMM... DIET BOOKS... DIET BOOKS... DIET BOOKS...
A-HA! DIET BOOKS! LET'S SEE WHAT THEY'VE GOT...

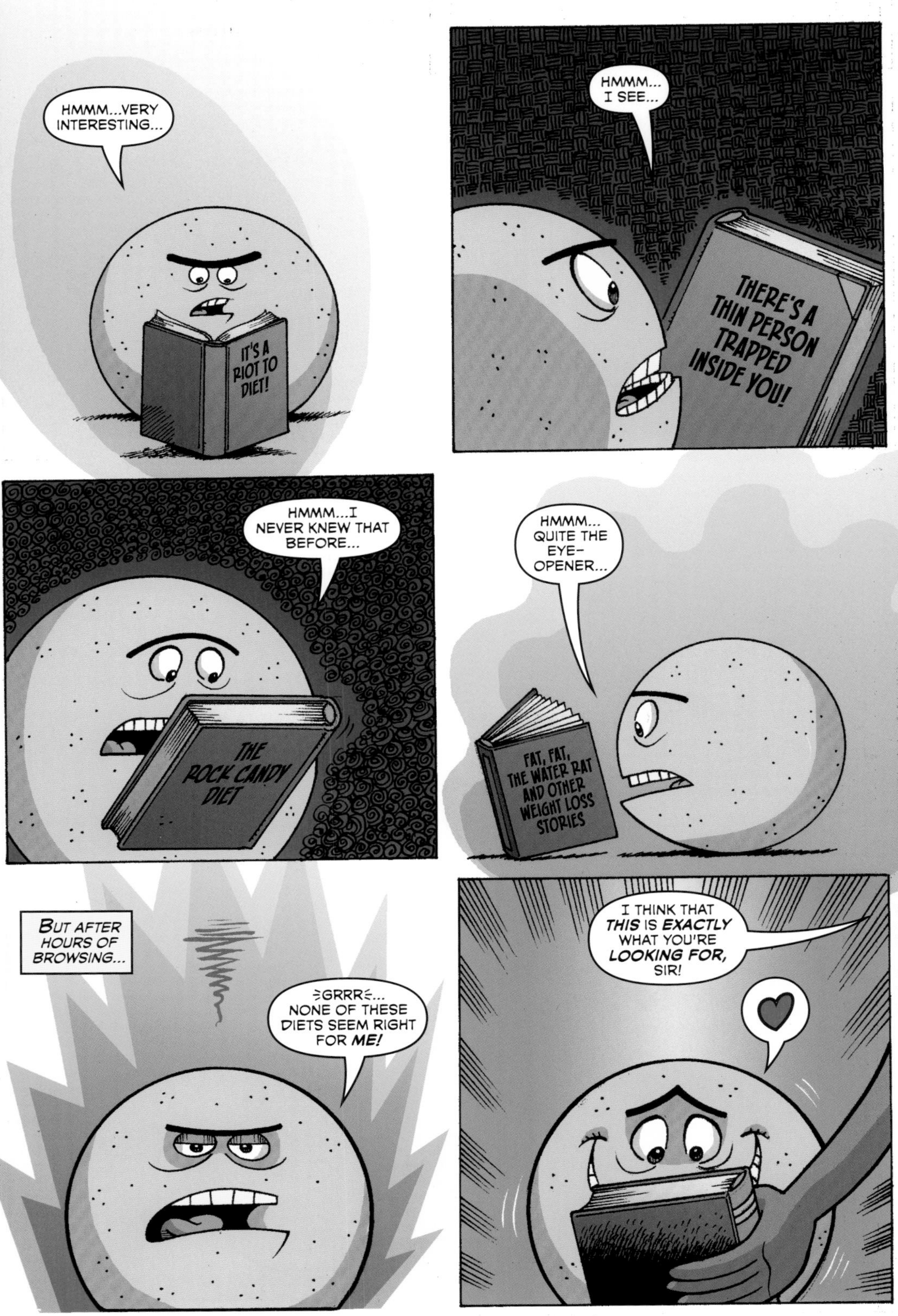
HMMM...VERY INTERESTING...
IT'S A RIOT TO DIET!
HMMM... I SEE...
THERE'S A THIN PERSON TRAPPED INSIDE YOU!
HMMM...I NEVER KNEW THAT BEFORE...
THE ROCK CANDY DIET
HMMM... QUITE THE EYE-OPENER...
FAT, FAT, THE WATER RAT AND OTHER WEIGHT LOSS STORIES
BUT AFTER HOURS OF BROWSING...
GRRR... NONE OF THESE DIETS SEEM RIGHT FOR ME!
I THINK THAT THIS IS EXACTLY WHAT YOU'RE LOOKING FOR, SIR!

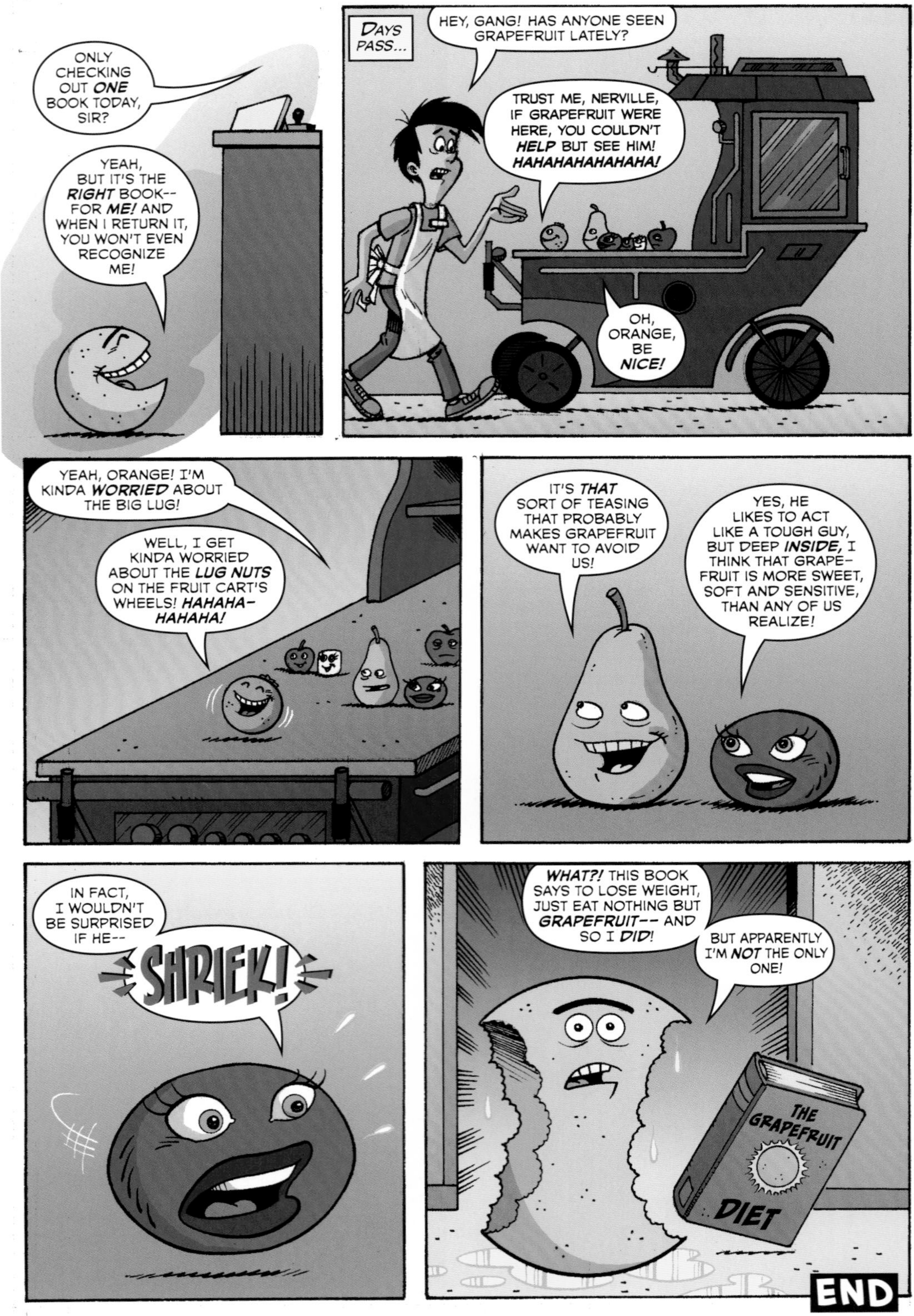
ONLY CHECKING OUT ONE BOOK TODAY, SIR?
YEAH, BUT IT'S THE RIGHT BOOK-- FOR ME! AND WHEN I RETURN IT, YOU WON'T EVEN RECOGNIZE ME!
DAYS PASS...
HEY, GANG! HAS ANYONE SEEN GRAPEFRUIT LATELY?
TRUST ME, NERVILLE, IF GRAPEFRUIT WERE HERE, YOU COULDN'T HELP BUT SEE HIM! HAHAHAHAHAHAHA!
OH, ORANGE, BE NICE!
YEAH, ORANGE! I'M KINDA WORRIED ABOUT THE BIG LUG!
WELL, I GET KINDA WORRIED ABOUT THE LUG NUTS ON THE FRUIT CART'S WHEELS! HAHAHA-HAHAHA!
IT'S THAT SORT OF TEASING THAT PROBABLY MAKES GRAPEFRUIT WANT TO AVOID US!
YES, HE LIKES TO ACT LIKE A TOUGH GUY, BUT DEEP INSIDE, I THINK THAT GRAPE-FRUIT IS MORE SWEET, SOFT AND SENSITIVE, THAN ANY OF US REALIZE!
IN FACT, I WOULDN'T BE SURPRISED IF HE--
SHRIEK!
WHAT?! THIS BOOK SAYS TO LOSE WEIGHT, JUST EAT NOTHING BUT GRAPEFRUIT-- AND SO I DID!
BUT APPARENTLY I'M NOT THE ONLY ONE!
THE GRAPEFRUIT DIET
END

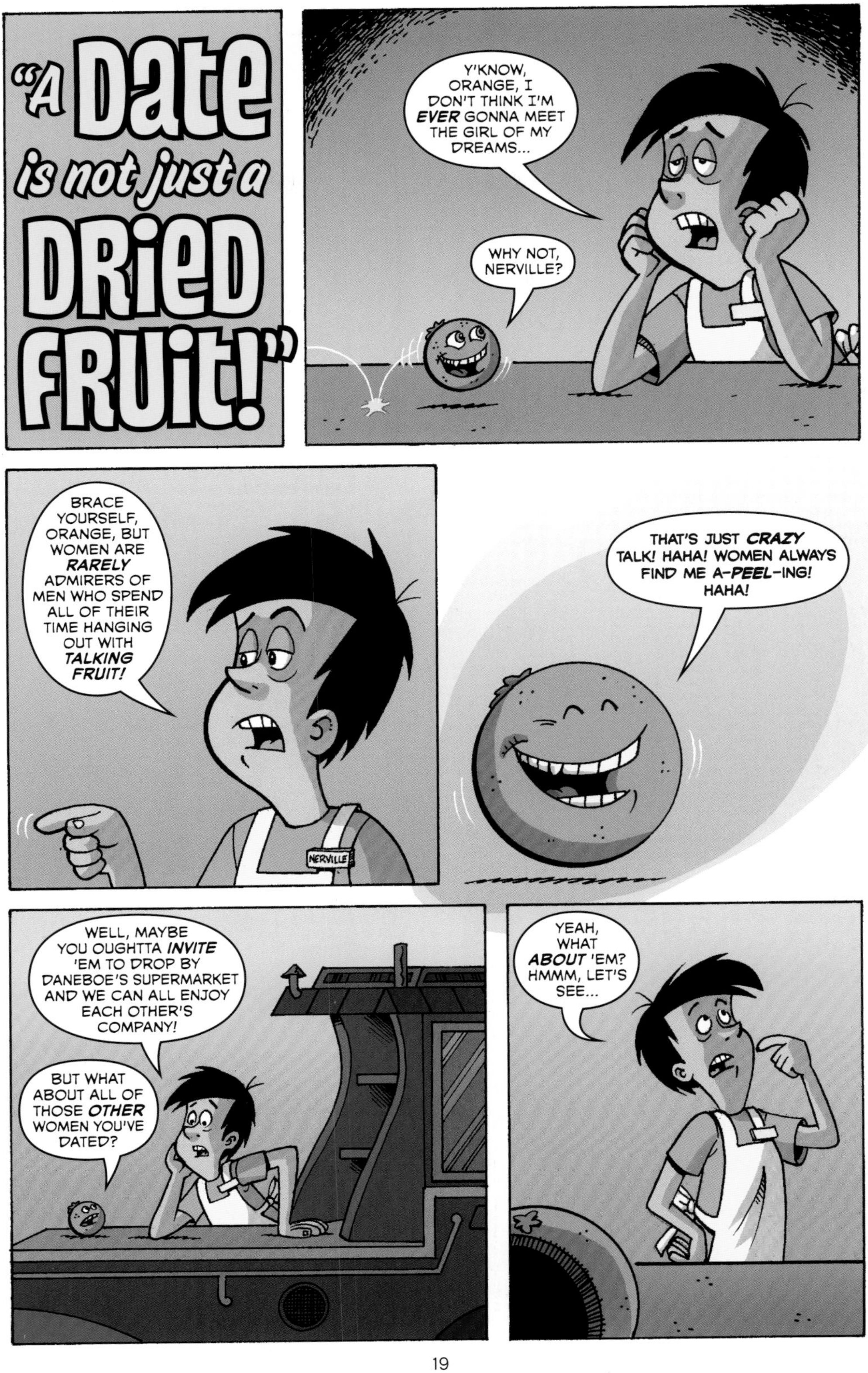
"A Date is not just a DRIED FRUIT!"
Y'KNOW, ORANGE, I DON'T THINK I'M EVER GONNA MEET THE GIRL OF MY DREAMS...
WHY NOT, NERVILLE?
BRACE YOURSELF, ORANGE, BUT WOMEN ARE RARELY ADMIRERS OF MEN WHO SPEND ALL OF THEIR TIME HANGING OUT WITH TALKING FRUIT!
NERVILLE
THAT'S JUST CRAZY TALK! HAHA! WOMEN ALWAYS FIND ME A-PEEL-ING! HAHA!
WELL, MAYBE YOU OUGHTTA INVITE 'EM TO DROP BY DANEBOE'S SUPERMARKET AND WE CAN ALL ENJOY EACH OTHER'S COMPANY!
BUT WHAT ABOUT ALL OF THOSE OTHER WOMEN YOU'VE DATED?
YEAH, WHAT ABOUT 'EM? HMMM, LET'S SEE...

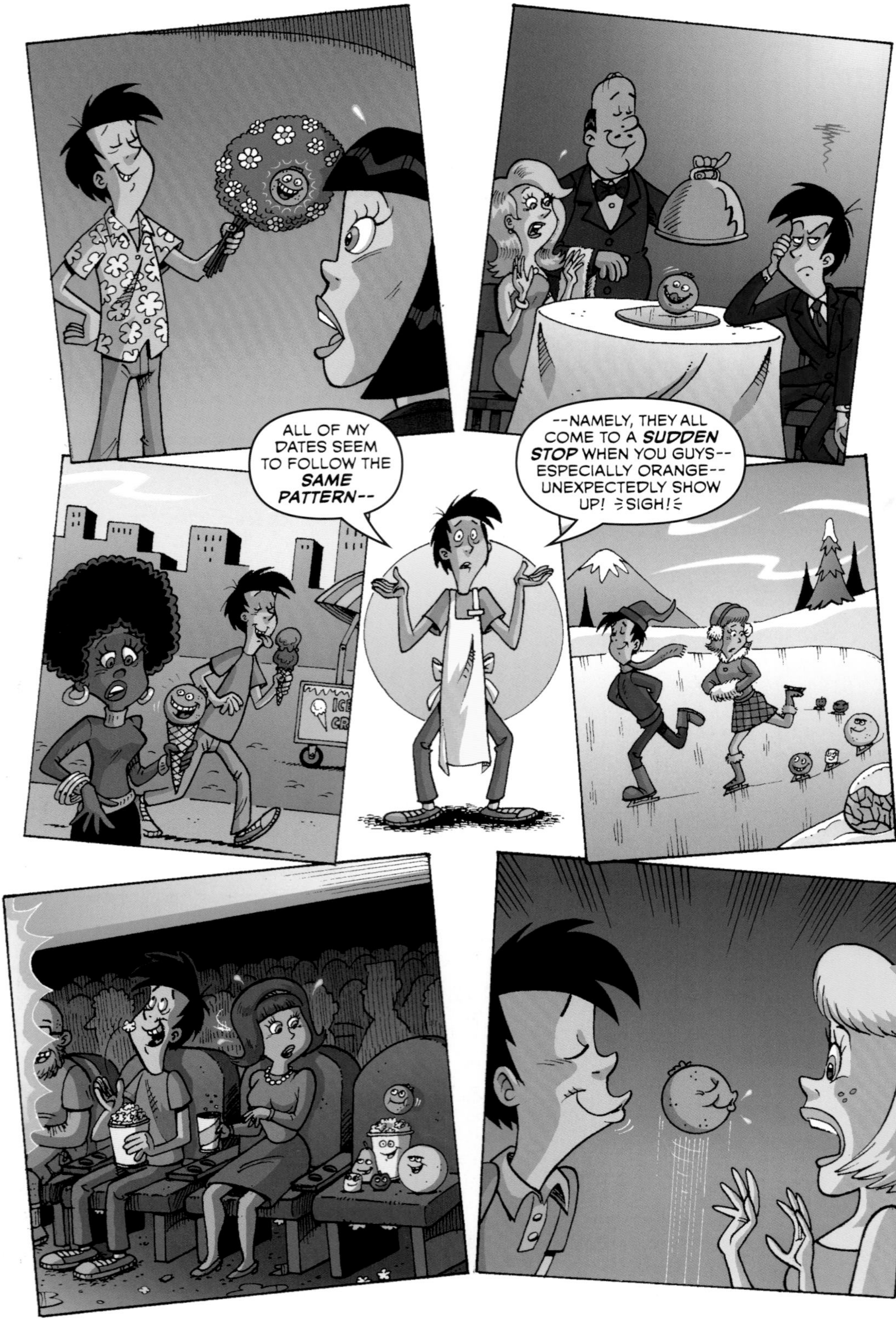
ALL OF MY DATES SEEM TO FOLLOW THE SAME PATTERN--
--NAMELY, THEY ALL COME TO A SUDDEN STOP WHEN YOU GUYS--ESPECIALLY ORANGE--UNEXPECTEDLY SHOW UP! ≥SIGH!≤
ICE
CR

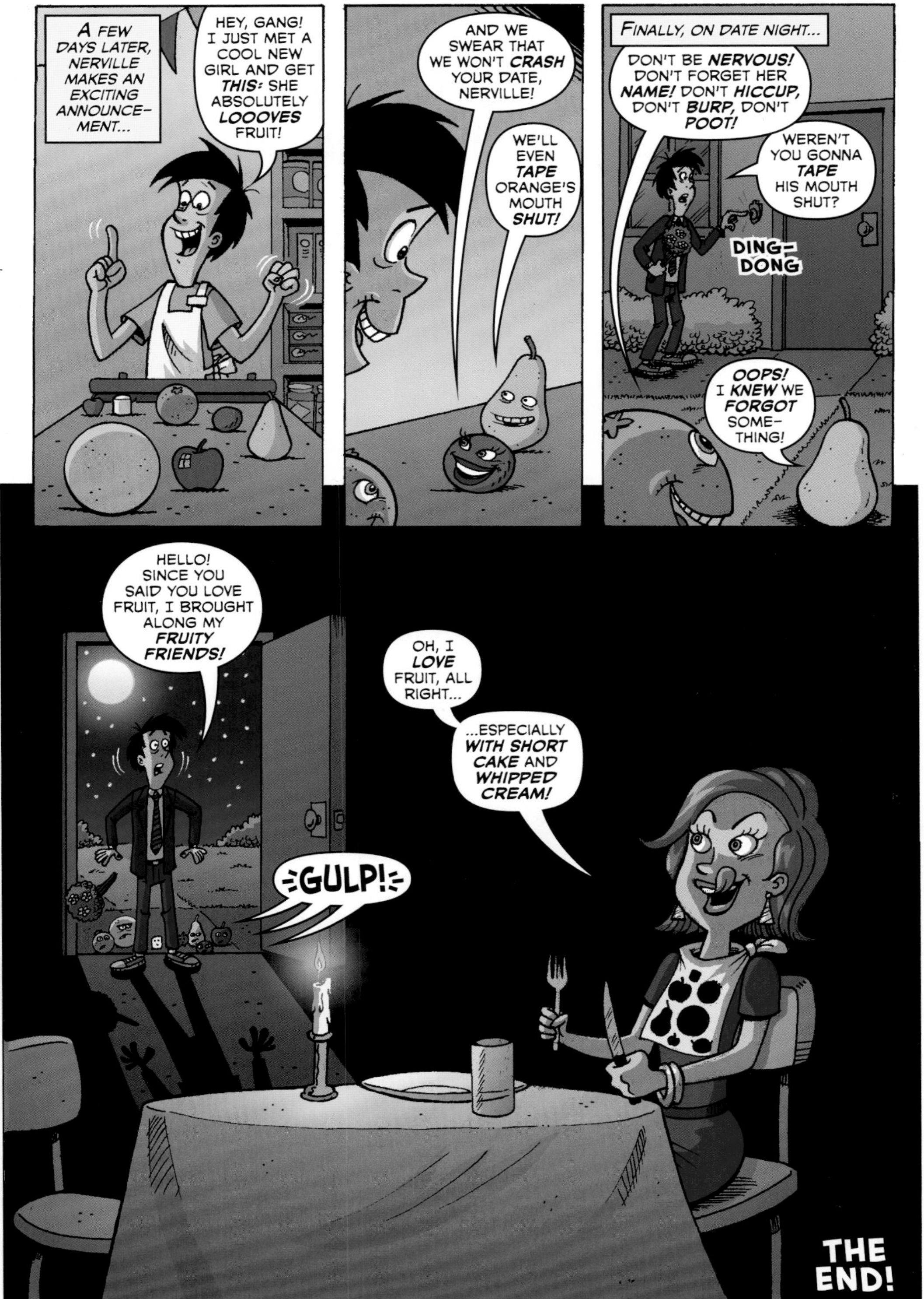
A FEW DAYS LATER, NERVILLE MAKES AN EXCITING ANNOUNCE-MENT...
HEY, GANG! I JUST MET A COOL NEW GIRL AND GET THIS: SHE ABSOLUTELY LOOOVES FRUIT!
AND WE SWEAR THAT WE WON'T CRASH YOUR DATE, NERVILLE!
WE'LL EVEN TAPE ORANGE'S MOUTH SHUT!
FINALLY, ON DATE NIGHT...
DON'T BE NERVOUS! DON'T FORGET HER NAME! DON'T HICCUP, DON'T BURP, DON'T POOT!
WEREN'T YOU GONNA TAPE HIS MOUTH SHUT?
DING-DONG
OOPS! I KNEW WE FORGOT SOME-THING!
HELLO! SINCE YOU SAID YOU LOVE FRUIT, I BROUGHT ALONG MY FRUITY FRIENDS!
OH, I LOVE FRUIT, ALL RIGHT...
...ESPECIALLY WITH SHORT CAKE AND WHIPPED CREAM!
GULP!
THE END!

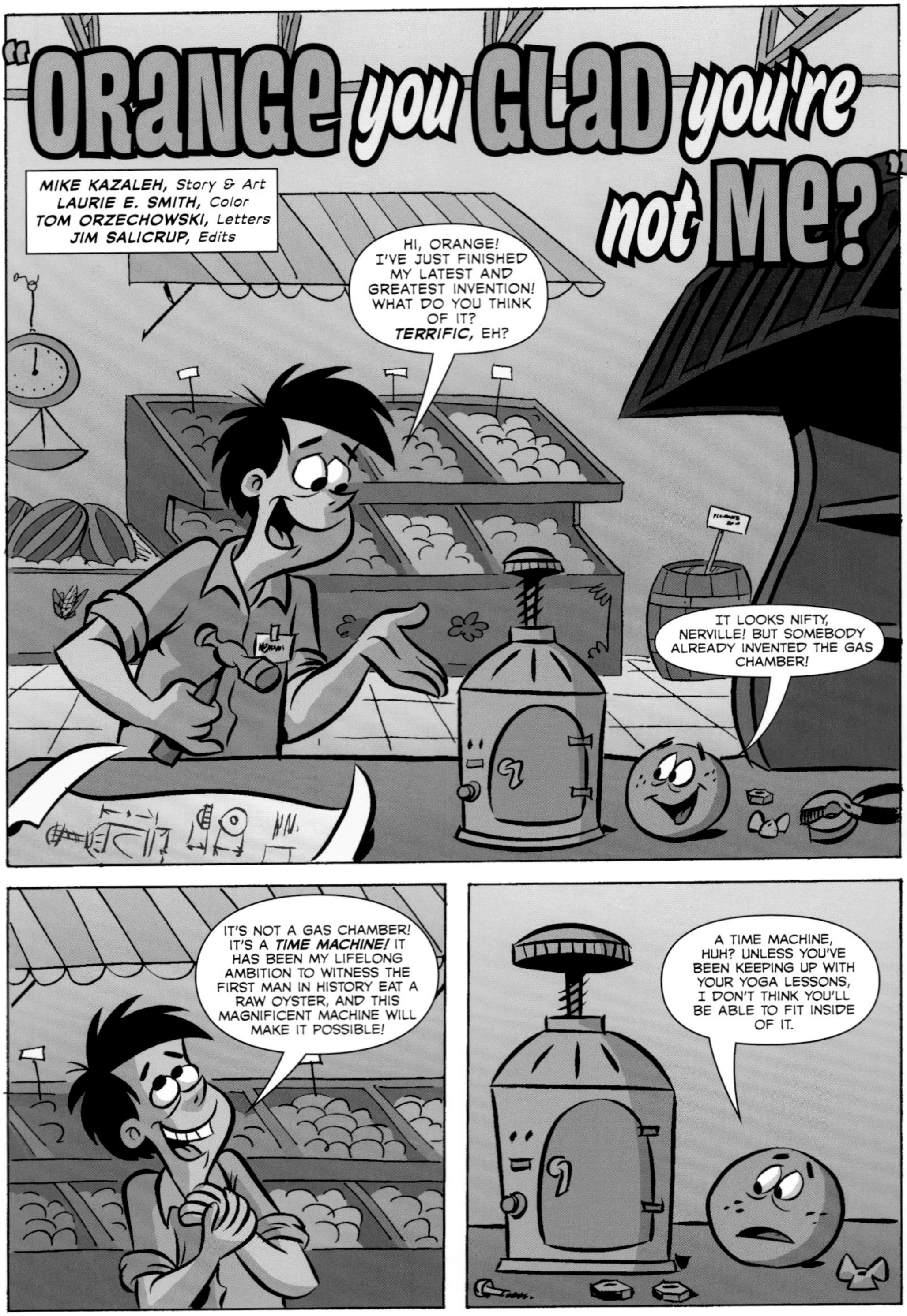
"ORANGE you GLAD you're not ME?"
MIKE KAZALEH, Story & Art
LAURIE E. SMITH, Color
TOM ORZECHOWSKI, Letters
JIM SALICRUP, Edits
HI, ORANGE! I'VE JUST FINISHED MY LATEST AND GREATEST INVENTION! WHAT DO YOU THINK OF IT? *TERRIFIC,* EH?
IT LOOKS NIFTY, NERVILLE! BUT SOMEBODY ALREADY INVENTED THE GAS CHAMBER!
IT'S NOT A GAS CHAMBER! IT'S A *TIME MACHINE!* IT HAS BEEN MY LIFELONG AMBITION TO WITNESS THE FIRST MAN IN HISTORY EAT A RAW OYSTER, AND THIS MAGNIFICENT MACHINE WILL MAKE IT POSSIBLE!
A TIME MACHINE, HUH? UNLESS YOU'VE BEEN KEEPING UP WITH YOUR YOGA LESSONS, I DON'T THINK YOU'LL BE ABLE TO FIT INSIDE OF IT.

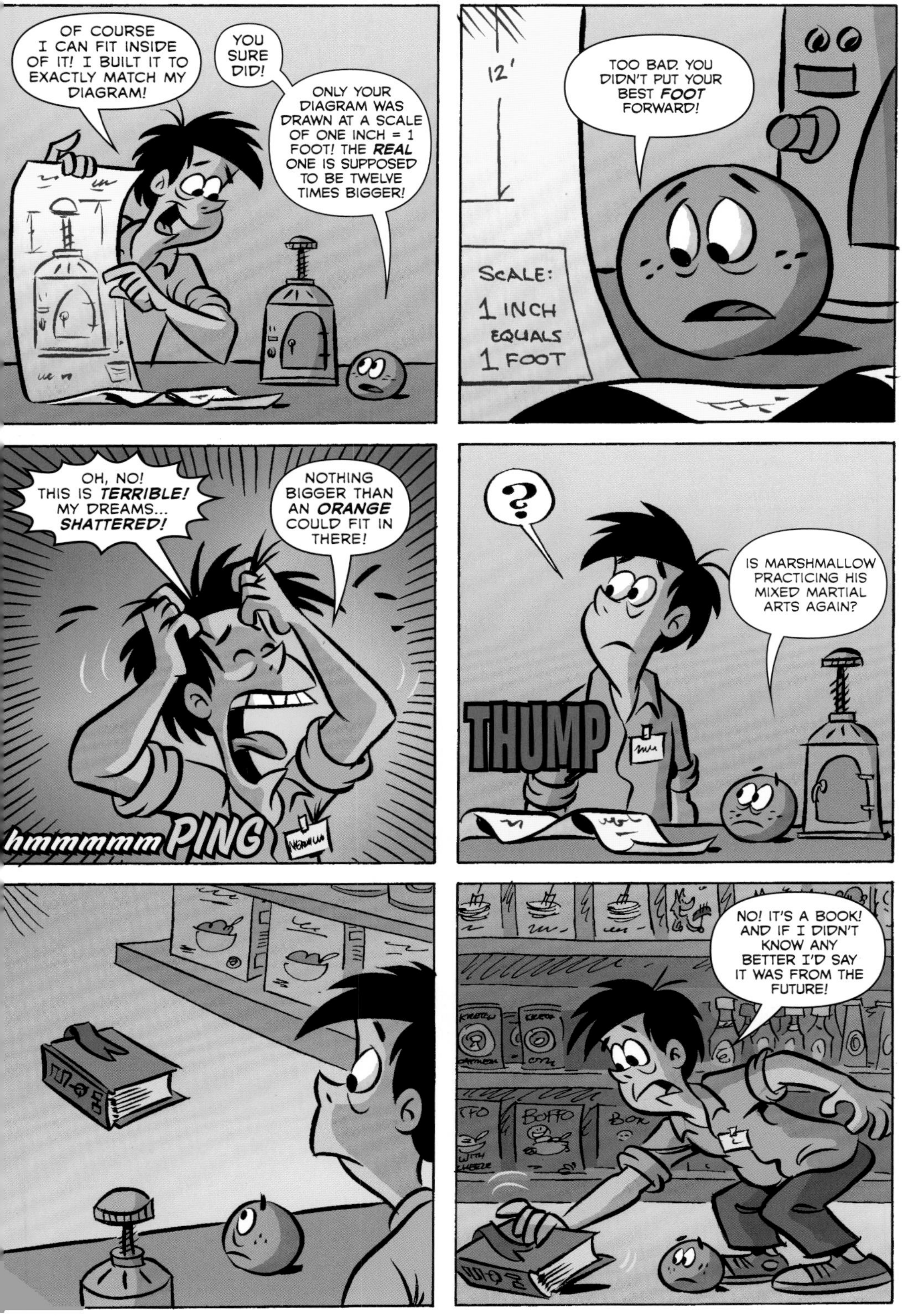
OF COURSE I CAN FIT INSIDE OF IT! I BUILT IT TO EXACTLY MATCH MY DIAGRAM!
YOU SURE DID!
ONLY YOUR DIAGRAM WAS DRAWN AT A SCALE OF ONE INCH = 1 FOOT! THE REAL ONE IS SUPPOSED TO BE TWELVE TIMES BIGGER!
12'
TOO BAD. YOU DIDN'T PUT YOUR BEST FOOT FORWARD!
SCALE: 1 INCH EQUALS 1 FOOT
OH, NO! THIS IS TERRIBLE! MY DREAMS... SHATTERED!
NOTHING BIGGER THAN AN ORANGE COULD FIT IN THERE!
hmmmmm PING
?
IS MARSHMALLOW PRACTICING HIS MIXED MARTIAL ARTS AGAIN?
THUMP
NO! IT'S A BOOK! AND IF I DIDN'T KNOW ANY BETTER I'D SAY IT WAS FROM THE FUTURE!
BOFFO

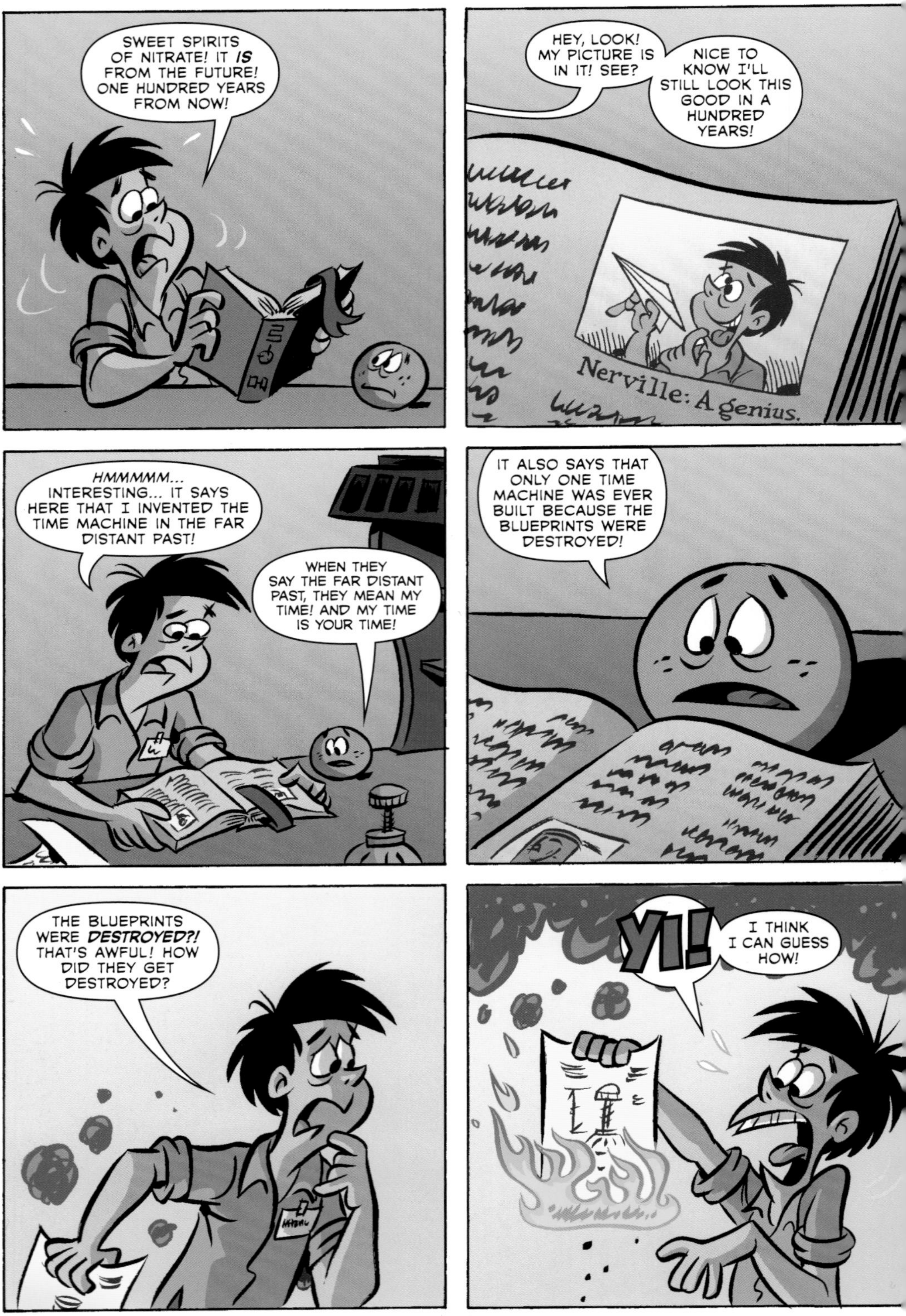

SWEET SPIRITS OF NITRATE! IT *IS* FROM THE FUTURE! ONE HUNDRED YEARS FROM NOW!
HEY, LOOK! MY PICTURE IS IN IT! SEE?
NICE TO KNOW I'LL STILL LOOK THIS GOOD IN A HUNDRED YEARS!
Nerville: A genius.
HMMMMM... INTERESTING... IT SAYS HERE THAT I INVENTED THE TIME MACHINE IN THE FAR DISTANT PAST!
WHEN THEY SAY THE FAR DISTANT PAST, THEY MEAN MY TIME! AND MY TIME IS YOUR TIME!
IT ALSO SAYS THAT ONLY ONE TIME MACHINE WAS EVER BUILT BECAUSE THE BLUEPRINTS WERE DESTROYED!
THE BLUEPRINTS WERE ***DESTROYED?!*** THAT'S AWFUL! HOW DID THEY GET DESTROYED?
YI!
I THINK I CAN GUESS HOW!

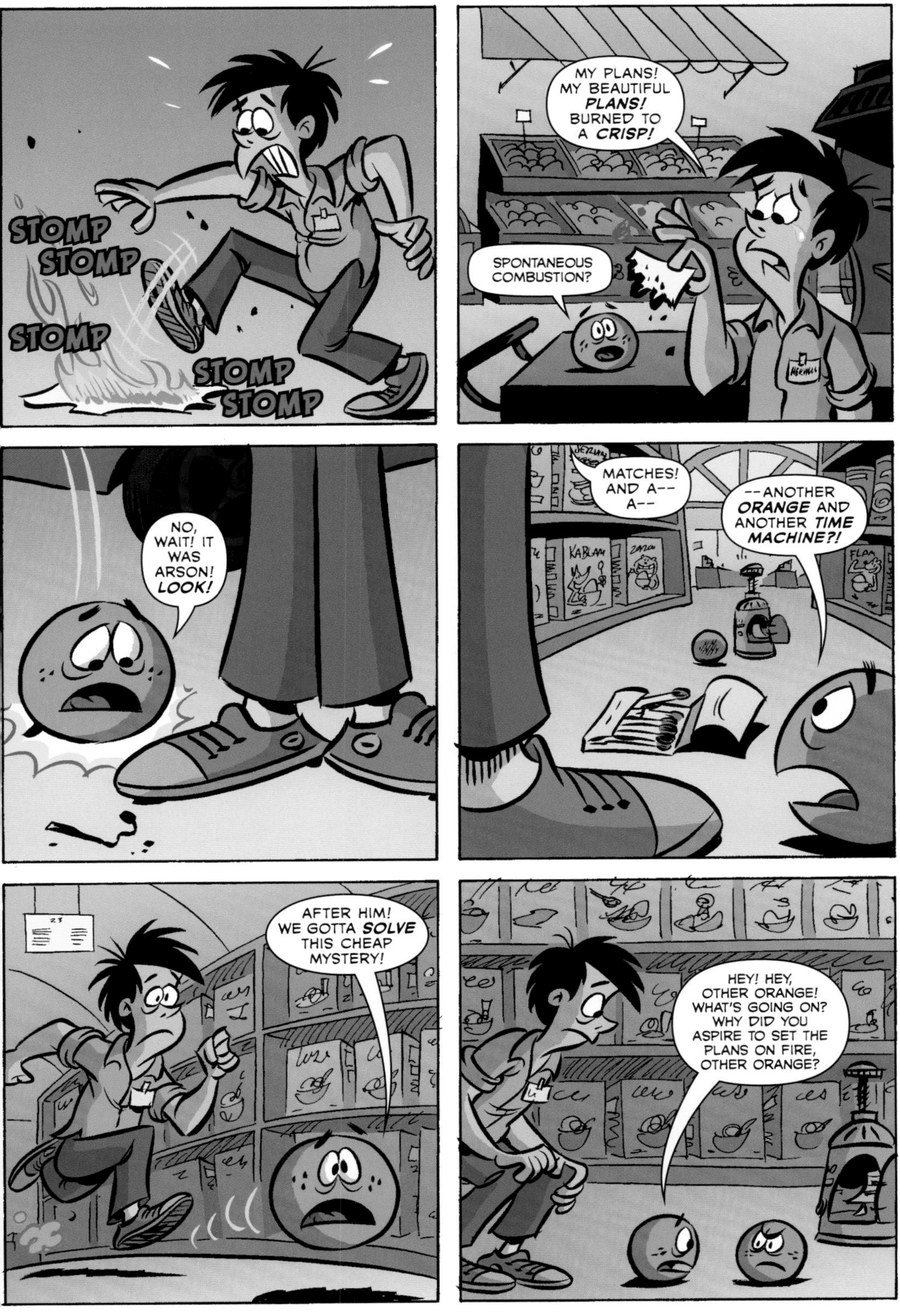
STOMP
STOMP
STOMP
STOMP
STOMP
MY PLANS! MY BEAUTIFUL PLANS! BURNED TO A CRISP!
SPONTANEOUS COMBUSTION?
NO, WAIT! IT WAS ARSON! LOOK!
MATCHES! AND A-- A--
--ANOTHER ORANGE AND ANOTHER TIME MACHINE?!
AFTER HIM! WE GOTTA SOLVE THIS CHEAP MYSTERY!
HEY! HEY, OTHER ORANGE! WHAT'S GOING ON? WHY DID YOU ASPIRE TO SET THE PLANS ON FIRE, OTHER ORANGE?

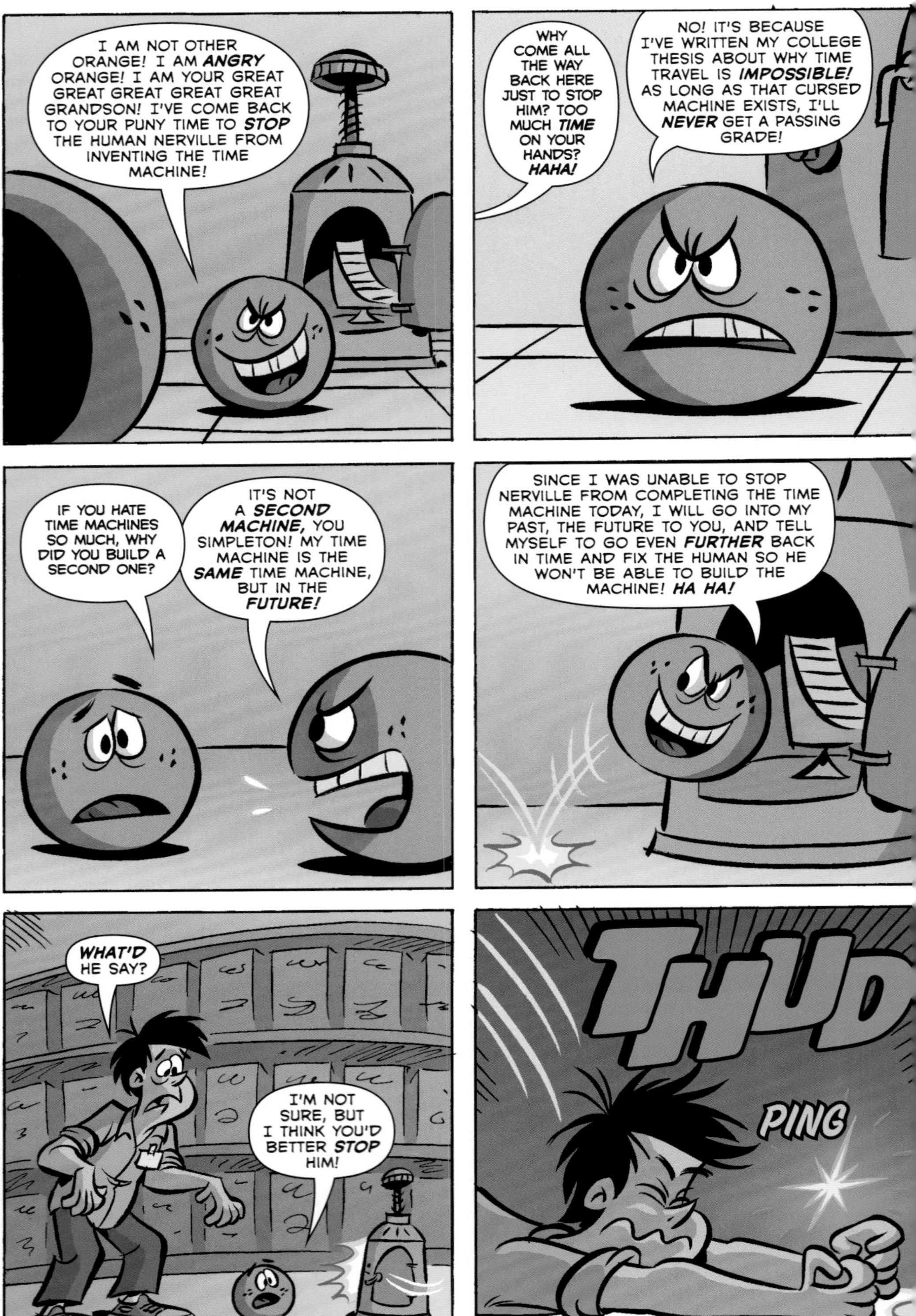
I AM NOT OTHER ORANGE! I AM **ANGRY** ORANGE! I AM YOUR GREAT GREAT GREAT GREAT GREAT GRANDSON! I'VE COME BACK TO YOUR PUNY TIME TO **STOP** THE HUMAN NERVILLE FROM INVENTING THE TIME MACHINE!
WHY COME ALL THE WAY BACK HERE JUST TO STOP HIM? TOO MUCH **TIME** ON YOUR HANDS? **HAHA!**
NO! IT'S BECAUSE I'VE WRITTEN MY COLLEGE THESIS ABOUT WHY TIME TRAVEL IS **IMPOSSIBLE!** AS LONG AS THAT CURSED MACHINE EXISTS, I'LL **NEVER** GET A PASSING GRADE!
IF YOU HATE TIME MACHINES SO MUCH, WHY DID YOU BUILD A SECOND ONE?
IT'S NOT A **SECOND MACHINE,** YOU SIMPLETON! MY TIME MACHINE IS THE **SAME** TIME MACHINE, BUT IN THE **FUTURE!**
SINCE I WAS UNABLE TO STOP NERVILLE FROM COMPLETING THE TIME MACHINE TODAY, I WILL GO INTO MY PAST, THE FUTURE TO YOU, AND TELL MYSELF TO GO EVEN **FURTHER** BACK IN TIME AND FIX THE HUMAN SO HE WON'T BE ABLE TO BUILD THE MACHINE! **HA HA!**
WHAT'D HE SAY?
I'M NOT SURE, BUT I THINK YOU'D BETTER **STOP** HIM!
THUD
PING

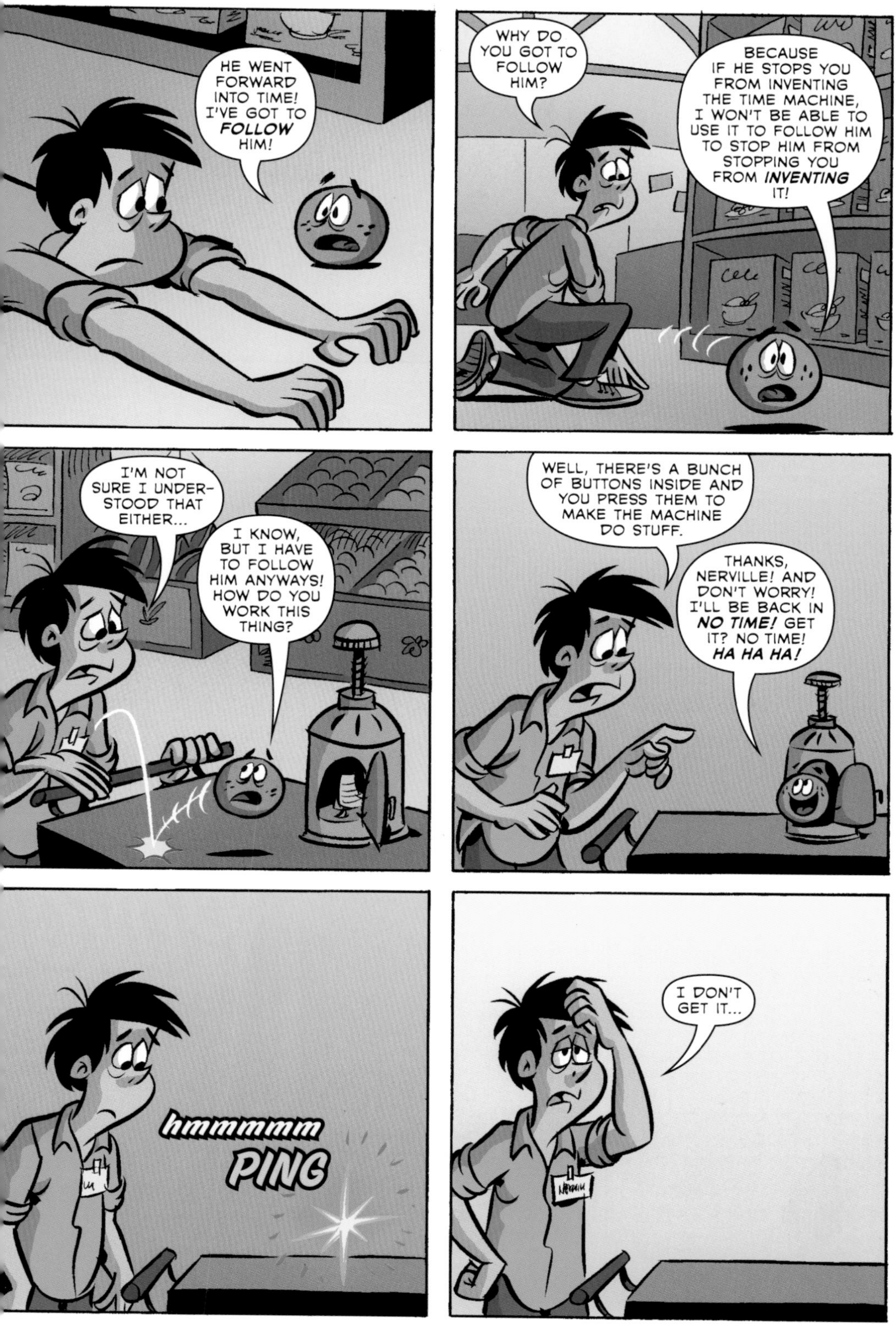
HE WENT FORWARD INTO TIME! I'VE GOT TO FOLLOW HIM!
WHY DO YOU GOT TO FOLLOW HIM?
BECAUSE IF HE STOPS YOU FROM INVENTING THE TIME MACHINE, I WON'T BE ABLE TO USE IT TO FOLLOW HIM TO STOP HIM FROM STOPPING YOU FROM INVENTING IT!
I'M NOT SURE I UNDERSTOOD THAT EITHER...
I KNOW, BUT I HAVE TO FOLLOW HIM ANYWAYS! HOW DO YOU WORK THIS THING?
WELL, THERE'S A BUNCH OF BUTTONS INSIDE AND YOU PRESS THEM TO MAKE THE MACHINE DO STUFF.
THANKS, NERVILLE! AND DON'T WORRY! I'LL BE BACK IN NO TIME! GET IT? NO TIME! HA HA HA!
hmmmmm
PING
I DON'T GET IT...

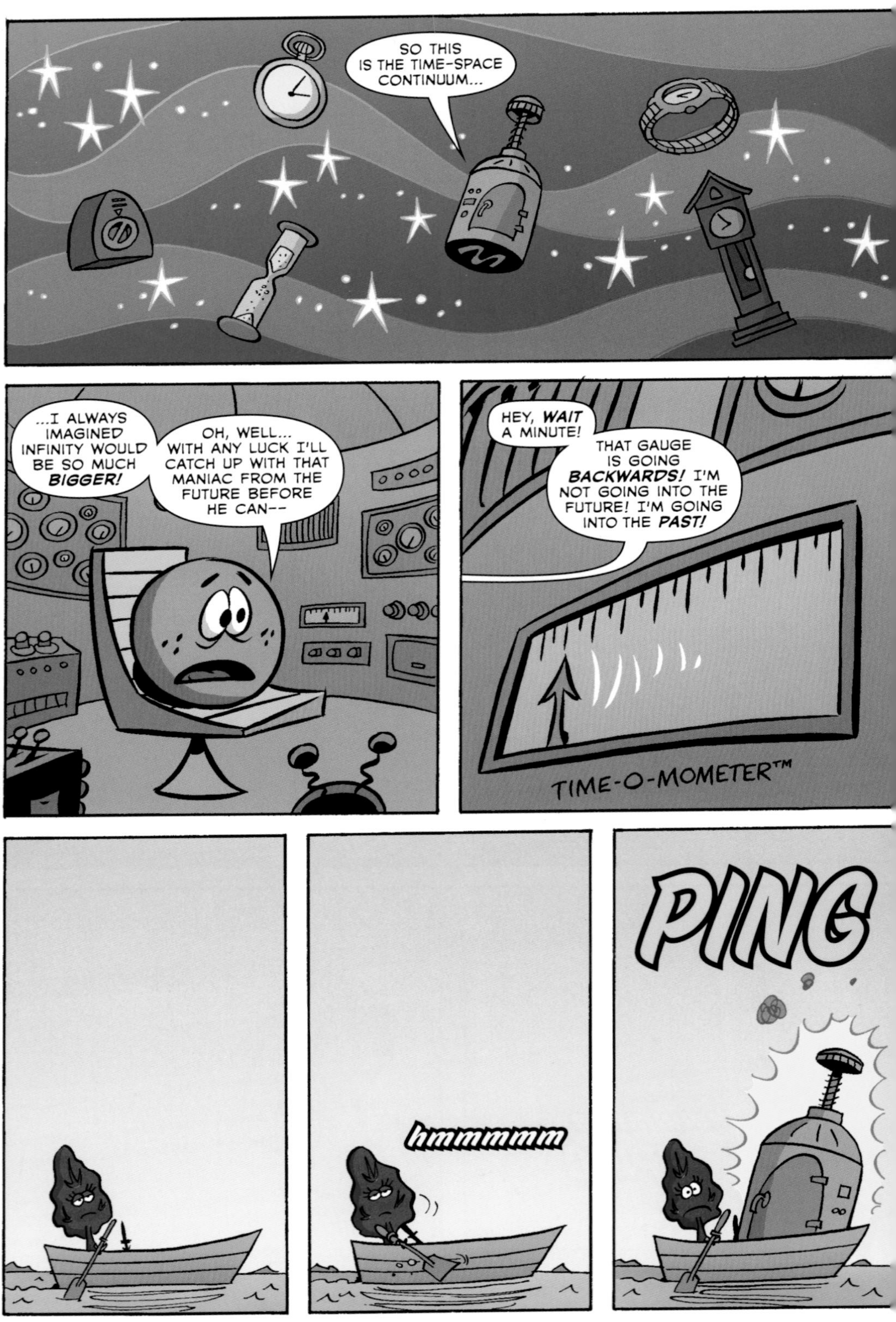
SO THIS IS THE TIME-SPACE CONTINUUM...
...I ALWAYS IMAGINED INFINITY WOULD BE SO MUCH BIGGER!
OH, WELL... WITH ANY LUCK I'LL CATCH UP WITH THAT MANIAC FROM THE FUTURE BEFORE HE CAN--
HEY, WAIT A MINUTE!
THAT GAUGE IS GOING BACKWARDS! I'M NOT GOING INTO THE FUTURE! I'M GOING INTO THE PAST!
TIME-O-MOMETER™
hmmmmmm
PING

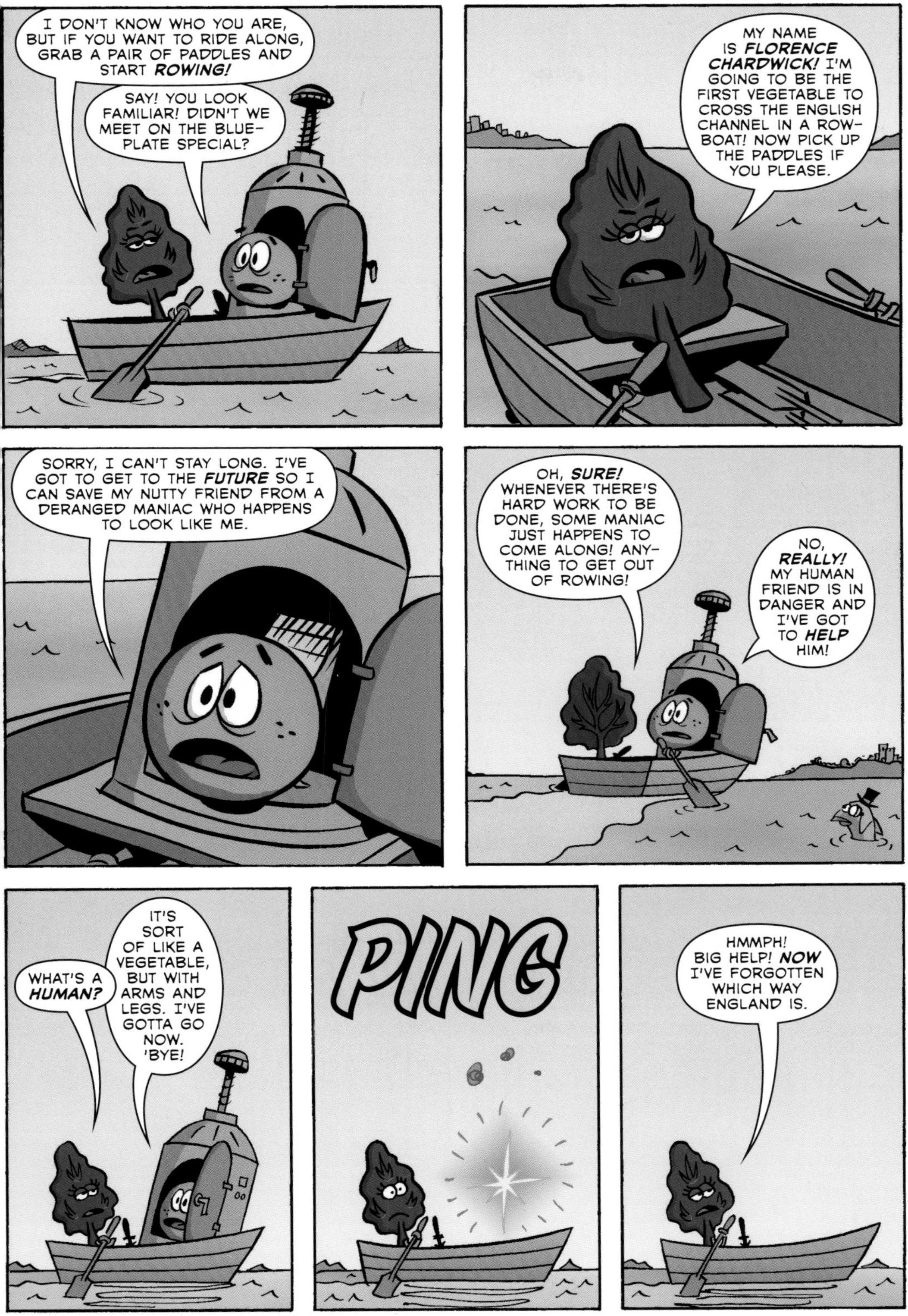
I DON'T KNOW WHO YOU ARE, BUT IF YOU WANT TO RIDE ALONG, GRAB A PAIR OF PADDLES AND START ROWING!
SAY! YOU LOOK FAMILIAR! DIDN'T WE MEET ON THE BLUE-PLATE SPECIAL?
MY NAME IS FLORENCE CHARDWICK! I'M GOING TO BE THE FIRST VEGETABLE TO CROSS THE ENGLISH CHANNEL IN A ROW-BOAT! NOW PICK UP THE PADDLES IF YOU PLEASE.
SORRY, I CAN'T STAY LONG. I'VE GOT TO GET TO THE FUTURE SO I CAN SAVE MY NUTTY FRIEND FROM A DERANGED MANIAC WHO HAPPENS TO LOOK LIKE ME.
OH, SURE! WHENEVER THERE'S HARD WORK TO BE DONE, SOME MANIAC JUST HAPPENS TO COME ALONG! ANY-THING TO GET OUT OF ROWING!
NO, REALLY! MY HUMAN FRIEND IS IN DANGER AND I'VE GOT TO HELP HIM!
WHAT'S A HUMAN?
IT'S SORT OF LIKE A VEGETABLE, BUT WITH ARMS AND LEGS. I'VE GOTTA GO NOW. 'BYE!
PING
HMMPH! BIG HELP! NOW I'VE FORGOTTEN WHICH WAY ENGLAND IS.

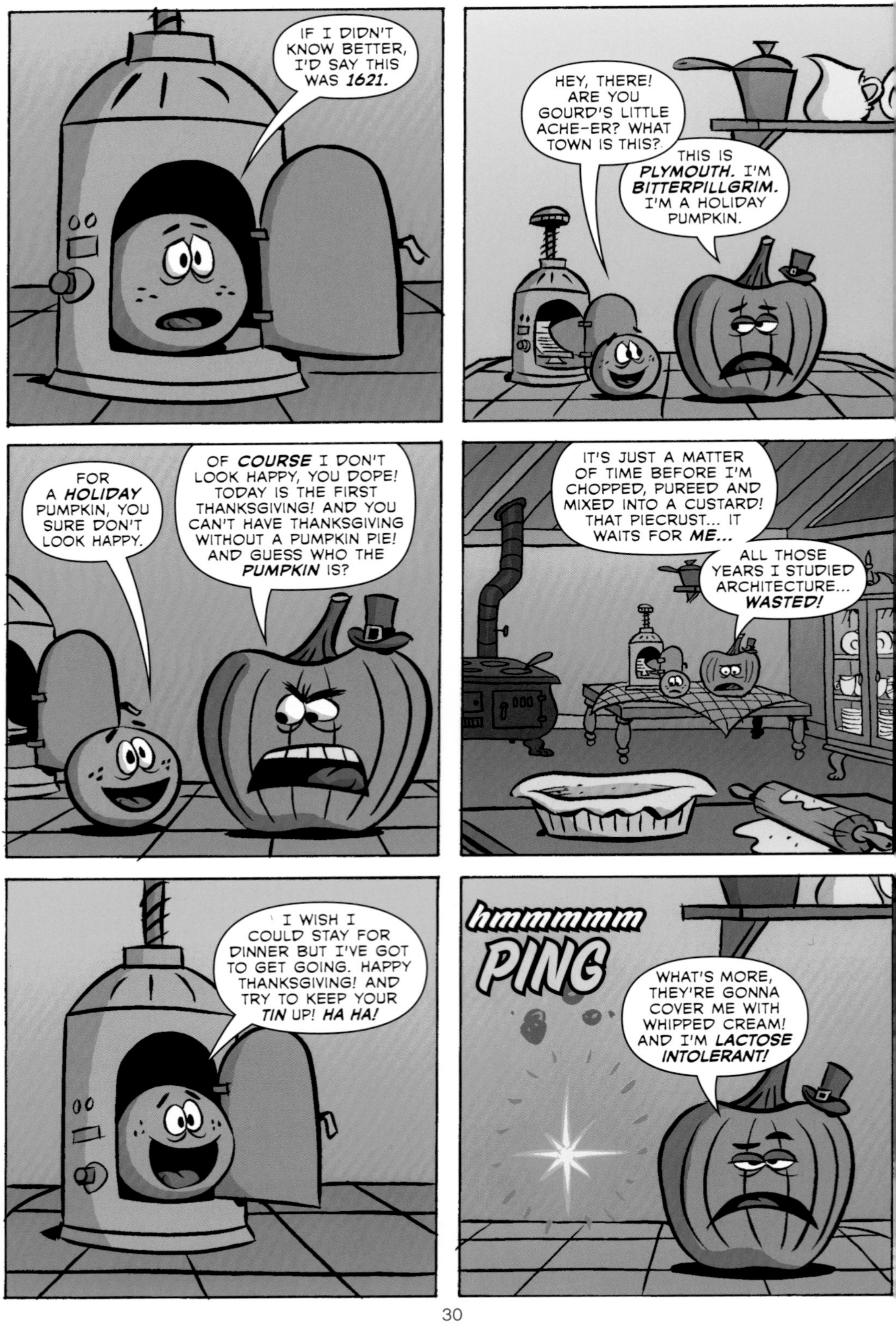
IF I DIDN'T KNOW BETTER, I'D SAY THIS WAS 1621.
HEY, THERE! ARE YOU GOURD'S LITTLE ACHE-ER? WHAT TOWN IS THIS?
THIS IS PLYMOUTH. I'M BITTERPILLGRIM. I'M A HOLIDAY PUMPKIN.
FOR A HOLIDAY PUMPKIN, YOU SURE DON'T LOOK HAPPY.
OF COURSE I DON'T LOOK HAPPY, YOU DOPE! TODAY IS THE FIRST THANKSGIVING! AND YOU CAN'T HAVE THANKSGIVING WITHOUT A PUMPKIN PIE! AND GUESS WHO THE PUMPKIN IS?
IT'S JUST A MATTER OF TIME BEFORE I'M CHOPPED, PUREED AND MIXED INTO A CUSTARD! THAT PIECRUST... IT WAITS FOR ME...
ALL THOSE YEARS I STUDIED ARCHITECTURE... WASTED!
I WISH I COULD STAY FOR DINNER BUT I'VE GOT TO GET GOING. HAPPY THANKSGIVING! AND TRY TO KEEP YOUR TIN UP! HA HA!
hmmmmmm
PING
WHAT'S MORE, THEY'RE GONNA COVER ME WITH WHIPPED CREAM! AND I'M LACTOSE INTOLERANT!

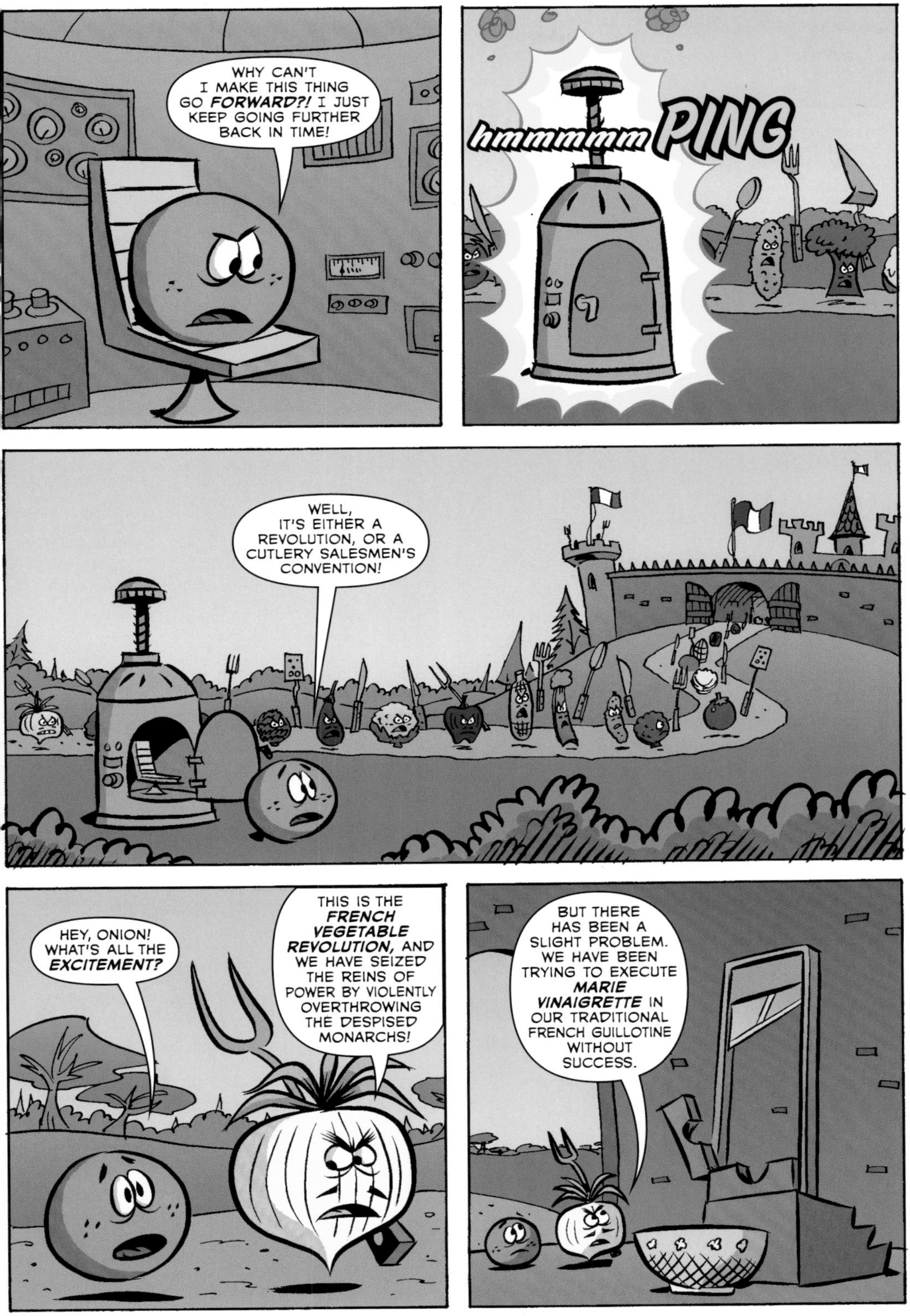
WHY CAN'T I MAKE THIS THING GO FORWARD?! I JUST KEEP GOING FURTHER BACK IN TIME!
hmmmmmm PING
WELL, IT'S EITHER A REVOLUTION, OR A CUTLERY SALESMEN'S CONVENTION!
HEY, ONION! WHAT'S ALL THE EXCITEMENT?
THIS IS THE FRENCH VEGETABLE REVOLUTION, AND WE HAVE SEIZED THE REINS OF POWER BY VIOLENTLY OVERTHROWING THE DESPISED MONARCHS!
BUT THERE HAS BEEN A SLIGHT PROBLEM. WE HAVE BEEN TRYING TO EXECUTE MARIE VINAIGRETTE IN OUR TRADITIONAL FRENCH GUILLOTINE WITHOUT SUCCESS.

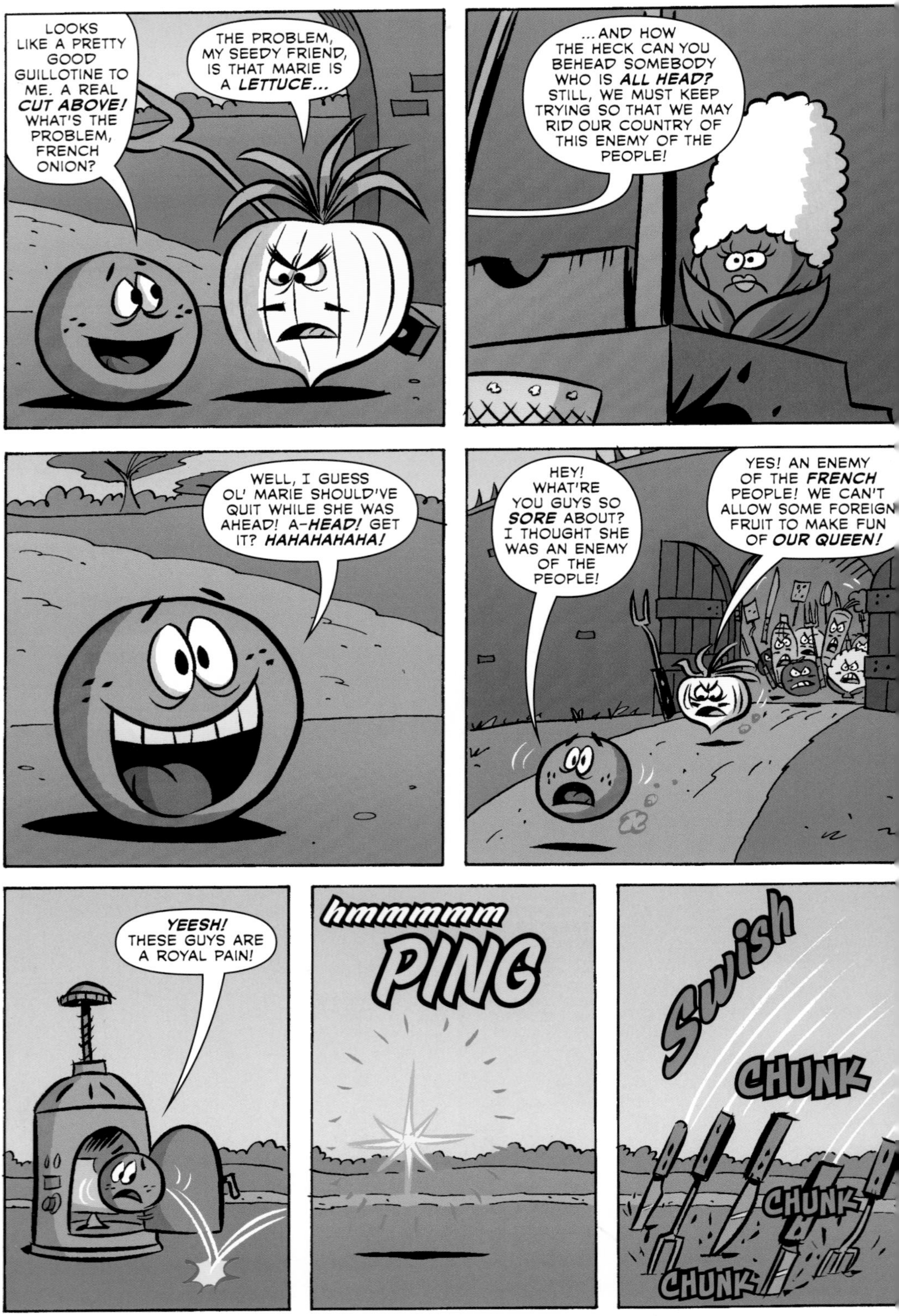
LOOKS LIKE A PRETTY GOOD GUILLOTINE TO ME. A REAL *CUT ABOVE!* WHAT'S THE PROBLEM, FRENCH ONION?
THE PROBLEM, MY SEEDY FRIEND, IS THAT MARIE IS A *LETTUCE...*
...AND HOW THE HECK CAN YOU BEHEAD SOMEBODY WHO IS *ALL HEAD?* STILL, WE MUST KEEP TRYING SO THAT WE MAY RID OUR COUNTRY OF THIS ENEMY OF THE PEOPLE!
WELL, I GUESS OL' MARIE SHOULD'VE QUIT WHILE SHE WAS AHEAD! A-*HEAD!* GET IT? *HAHAHAHAHA!*
HEY! WHAT'RE YOU GUYS SO *SORE* ABOUT? I THOUGHT SHE WAS AN ENEMY OF THE PEOPLE!
YES! AN ENEMY OF THE *FRENCH* PEOPLE! WE CAN'T ALLOW SOME FOREIGN FRUIT TO MAKE FUN OF *OUR QUEEN!*
YEESH! THESE GUYS ARE A ROYAL PAIN!
hmmmmmm
PING
Swish
CHUNK
CHUNK
CHUNK

Welcome to
RoMA ToMATo
ROTISSERIE
Lions
HMMMM... SOMEBODY MUST BE HAVING A BARBEQUE...
HEY! HEY, PICKLE! YOU'D BETTER GET OUT OF HERE! YOUR TOWN IS ON FIRE!
GET OUT OF HERE?! IN THE MIDDLE OF A JAM SESSION?! YOU MUST BE MAD!
I AM EMPEROR SPEAR-O, AND I BLOW FLUGEL-HORN!
I'VE GOT A REAL SWINGIN' GROUP, TOO! I CALL THEM MY HOT FIVE!
IF YOU MEAN THOSE ROASTED PEPPERS OVER THERE, THEY LOOK HOT, ALL RIGHT.
OH, BAZZ FAZZ! LOOKS LIKE OL' SPEAR-O IS DOING A SOLO TONIGHT!
UNLESS YOU'D LIKE TO MAKE IT A DUET! WHAT DO YOU BLOW?
THE SCENE! THIS IS TOO HOT FOR ME!
THIS IS RIDICULOUS! I'M STILL GOING BACKWARDS! WHERE WILL I END UP NEXT?!

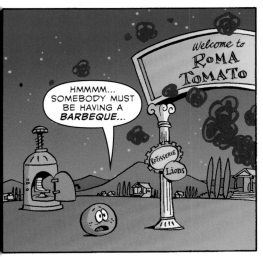

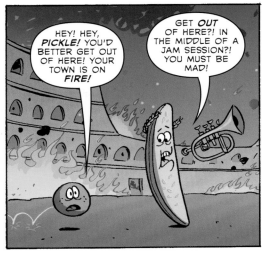

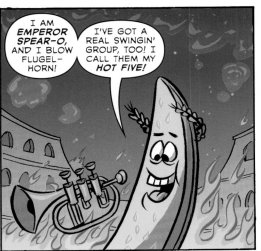

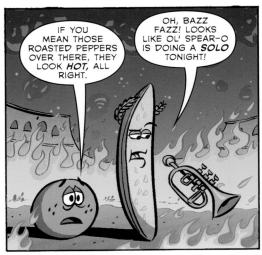

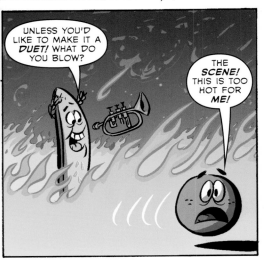

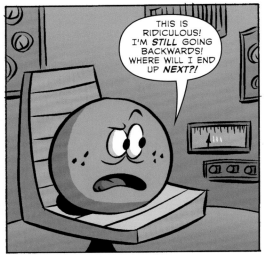

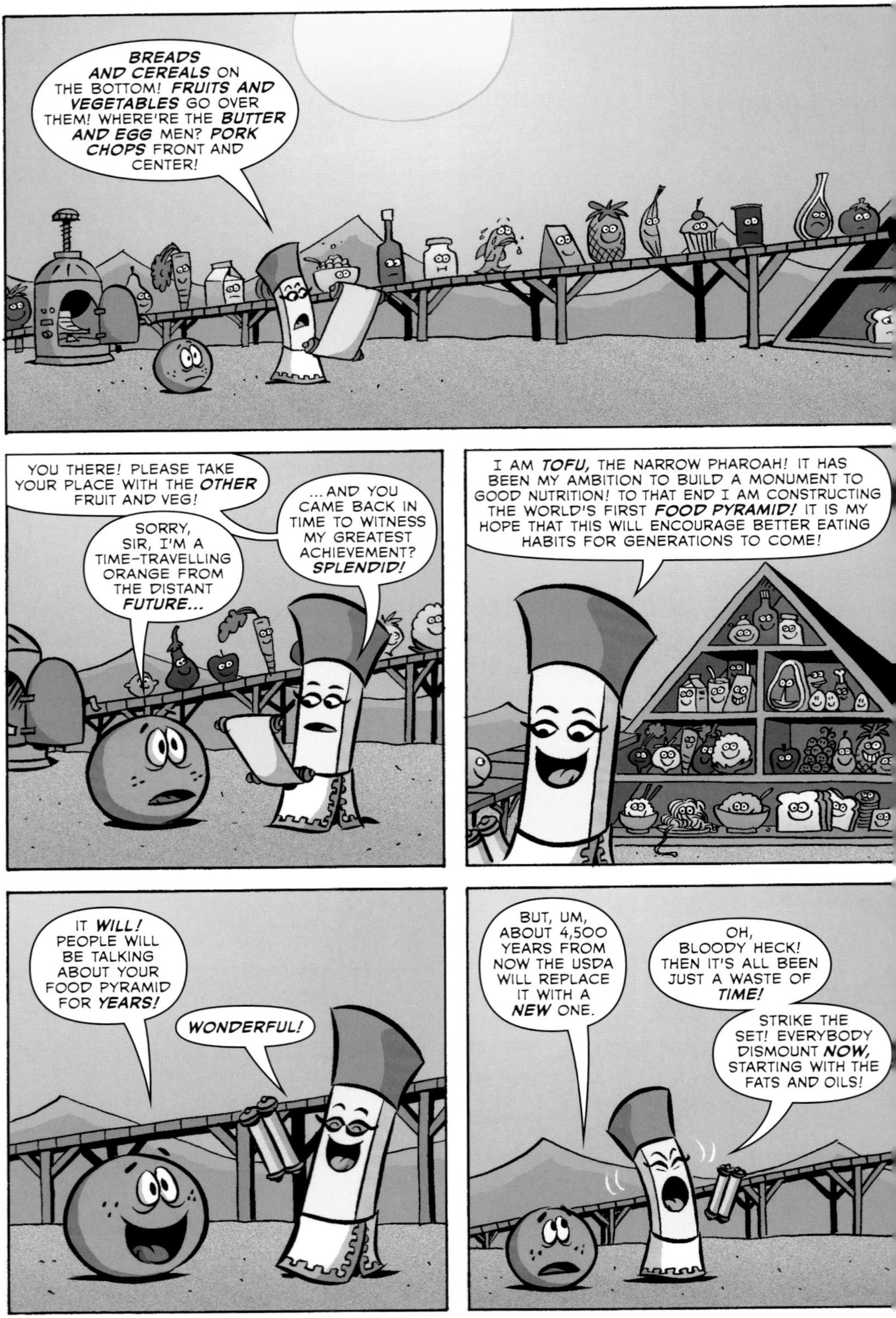
BREADS AND CEREALS ON THE BOTTOM! FRUITS AND VEGETABLES GO OVER THEM! WHERE'RE THE BUTTER AND EGG MEN? PORK CHOPS FRONT AND CENTER!
YOU THERE! PLEASE TAKE YOUR PLACE WITH THE OTHER FRUIT AND VEG!
SORRY, SIR, I'M A TIME-TRAVELLING ORANGE FROM THE DISTANT FUTURE...
...AND YOU CAME BACK IN TIME TO WITNESS MY GREATEST ACHIEVEMENT? SPLENDID!
I AM TOFU, THE NARROW PHAROAH! IT HAS BEEN MY AMBITION TO BUILD A MONUMENT TO GOOD NUTRITION! TO THAT END I AM CONSTRUCTING THE WORLD'S FIRST FOOD PYRAMID! IT IS MY HOPE THAT THIS WILL ENCOURAGE BETTER EATING HABITS FOR GENERATIONS TO COME!
IT WILL! PEOPLE WILL BE TALKING ABOUT YOUR FOOD PYRAMID FOR YEARS!
WONDERFUL!
BUT, UM, ABOUT 4,500 YEARS FROM NOW THE USDA WILL REPLACE IT WITH A NEW ONE.
OH, BLOODY HECK! THEN IT'S ALL BEEN JUST A WASTE OF TIME!
STRIKE THE SET! EVERYBODY DISMOUNT NOW, STARTING WITH THE FATS AND OILS!

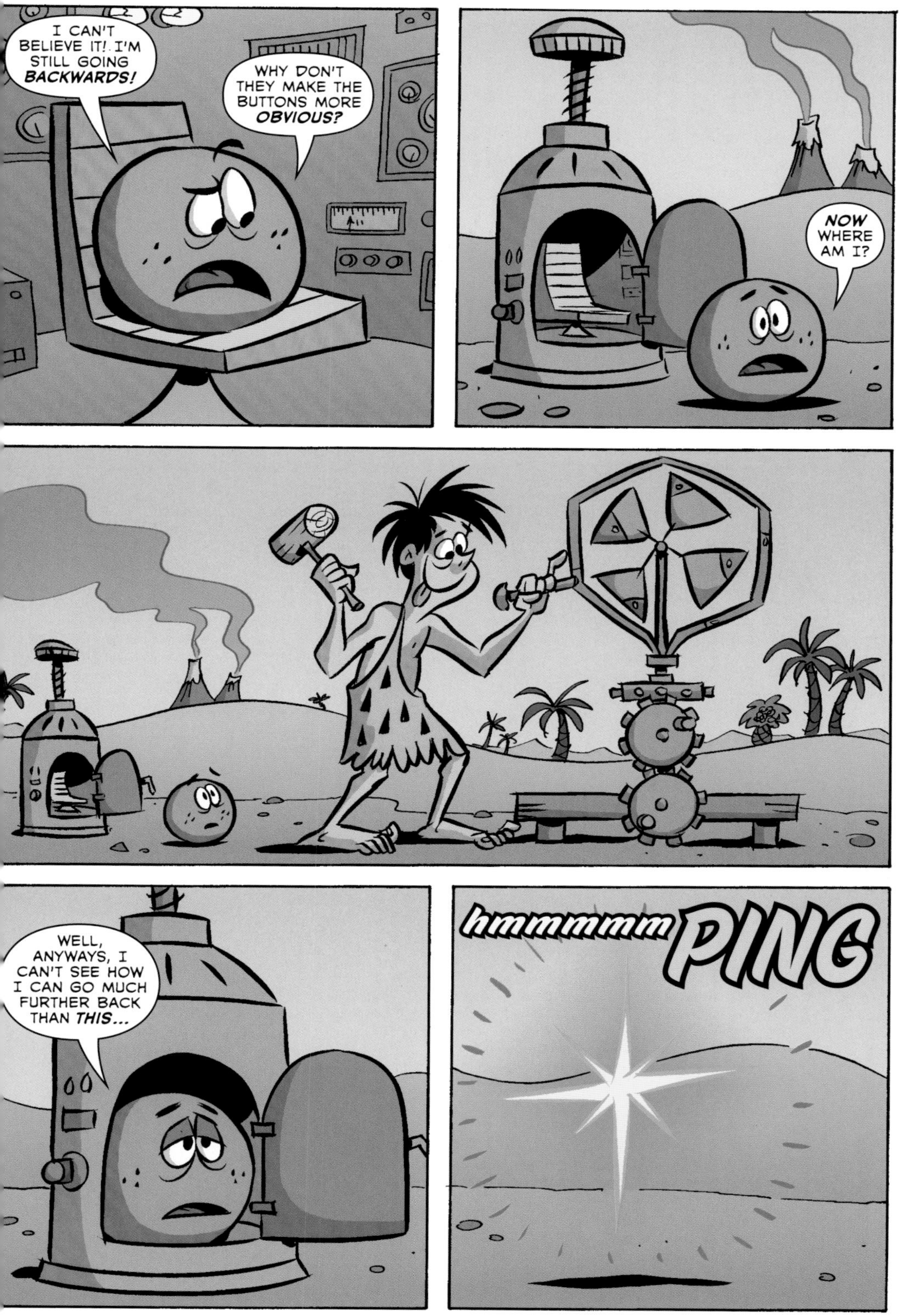
I CAN'T BELIEVE IT! I'M STILL GOING BACKWARDS!
WHY DON'T THEY MAKE THE BUTTONS MORE OBVIOUS?
NOW WHERE AM I?
WELL, ANYWAYS, I CAN'T SEE HOW I CAN GO MUCH FURTHER BACK THAN THIS...
hmmmmmm PING

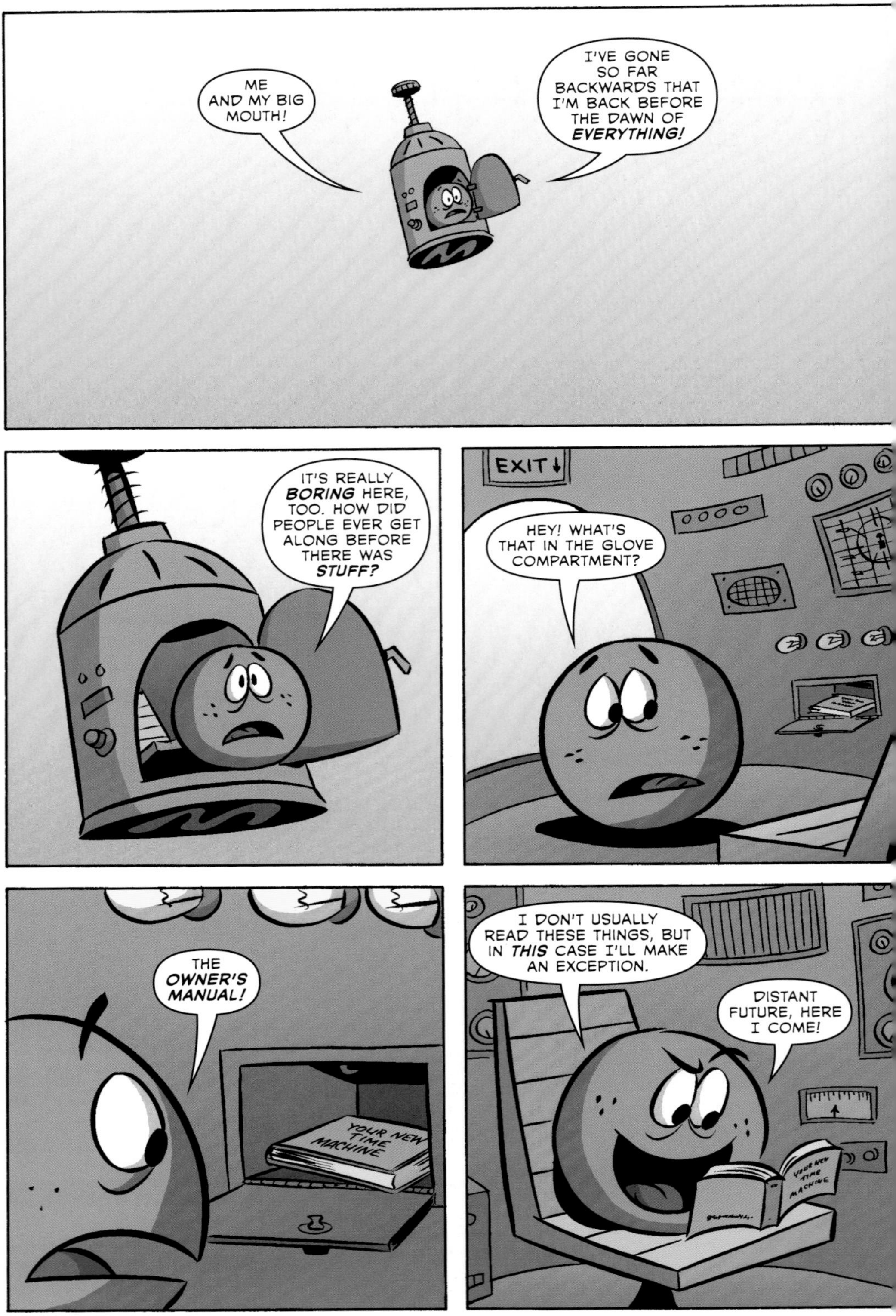
ME AND MY BIG MOUTH!
I'VE GONE SO FAR BACKWARDS THAT I'M BACK BEFORE THE DAWN OF *EVERYTHING!*
IT'S REALLY *BORING* HERE, TOO. HOW DID PEOPLE EVER GET ALONG BEFORE THERE WAS *STUFF?*
EXIT
HEY! WHAT'S THAT IN THE GLOVE COMPARTMENT?
THE *OWNER'S MANUAL!*
YOUR NEW TIME MACHINE
I DON'T USUALLY READ THESE THINGS, BUT IN *THIS* CASE I'LL MAKE AN EXCEPTION.
DISTANT FUTURE, HERE I COME!
YOUR NEW TIME MACHINE

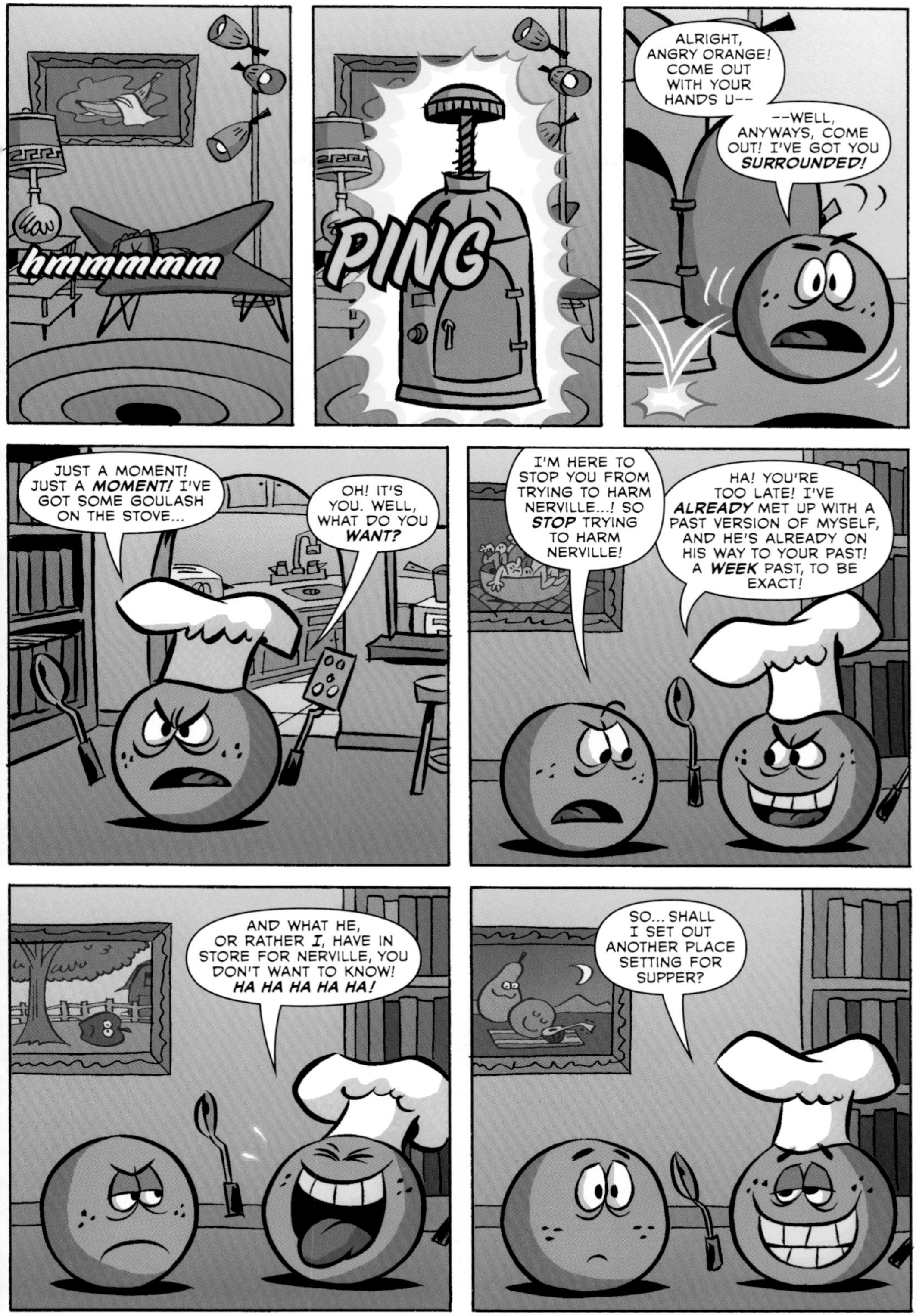
hmmmmm
PING
ALRIGHT, ANGRY ORANGE! COME OUT WITH YOUR HANDS U--
--WELL, ANYWAYS, COME OUT! I'VE GOT YOU SURROUNDED!
JUST A MOMENT! JUST A MOMENT! I'VE GOT SOME GOULASH ON THE STOVE...
OH! IT'S YOU. WELL, WHAT DO YOU WANT?
I'M HERE TO STOP YOU FROM TRYING TO HARM NERVILLE...! SO STOP TRYING TO HARM NERVILLE!
HA! YOU'RE TOO LATE! I'VE ALREADY MET UP WITH A PAST VERSION OF MYSELF, AND HE'S ALREADY ON HIS WAY TO YOUR PAST! A WEEK PAST, TO BE EXACT!
AND WHAT HE, OR RATHER I, HAVE IN STORE FOR NERVILLE, YOU DON'T WANT TO KNOW! HA HA HA HA HA!
SO... SHALL I SET OUT ANOTHER PLACE SETTING FOR SUPPER?

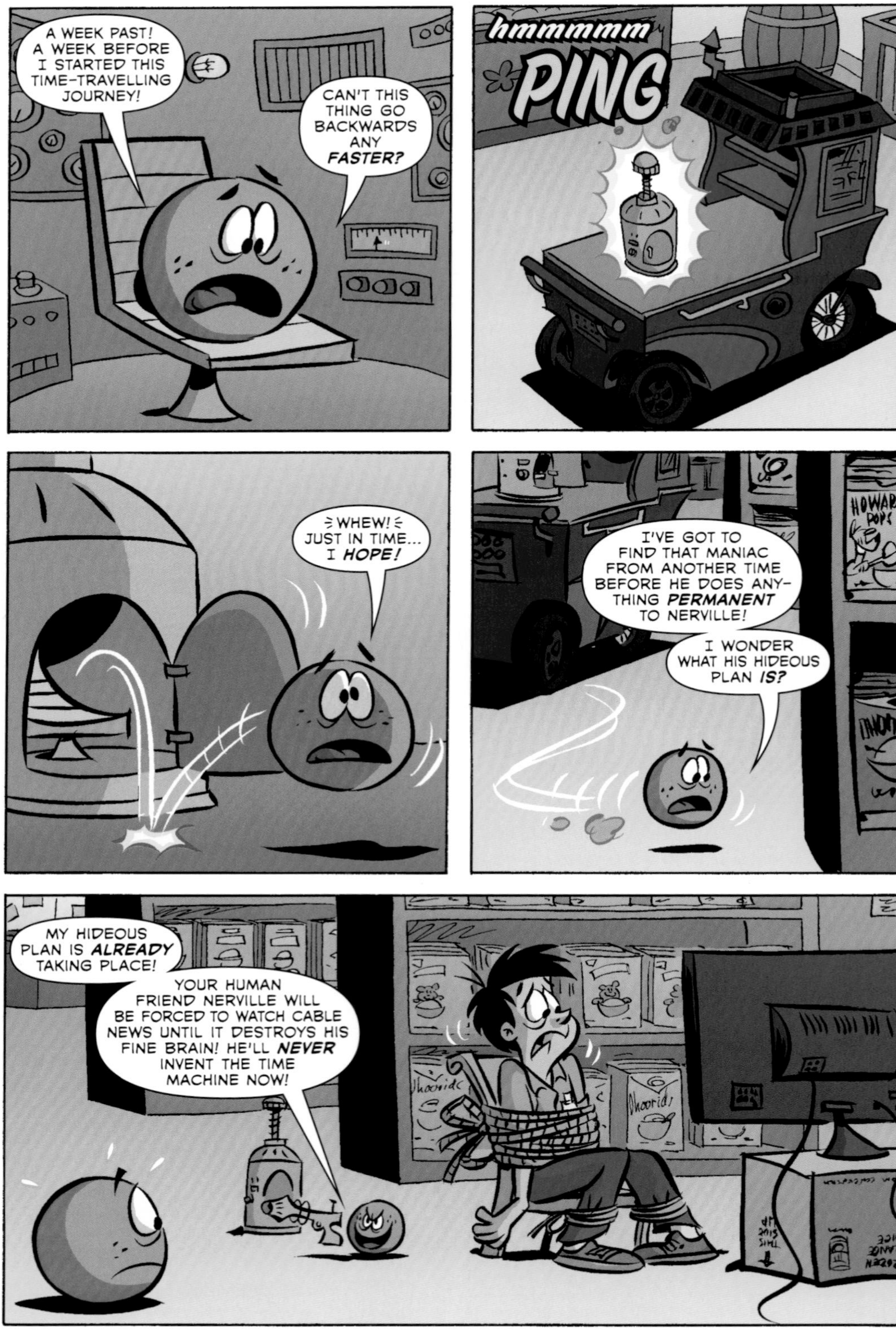
A WEEK PAST! A WEEK BEFORE I STARTED THIS TIME-TRAVELLING JOURNEY!
CAN'T THIS THING GO BACKWARDS ANY *FASTER?*
hmmmmm
PING
WHEW! JUST IN TIME... I *HOPE!*
I'VE GOT TO FIND THAT MANIAC FROM ANOTHER TIME BEFORE HE DOES ANY-THING *PERMANENT* TO NERVILLE!
I WONDER WHAT HIS HIDEOUS PLAN *IS?*
HOWARD POPS
MY HIDEOUS PLAN IS *ALREADY* TAKING PLACE!
YOUR HUMAN FRIEND NERVILLE WILL BE FORCED TO WATCH CABLE NEWS UNTIL IT DESTROYS HIS FINE BRAIN! HE'LL *NEVER* INVENT THE TIME MACHINE NOW!

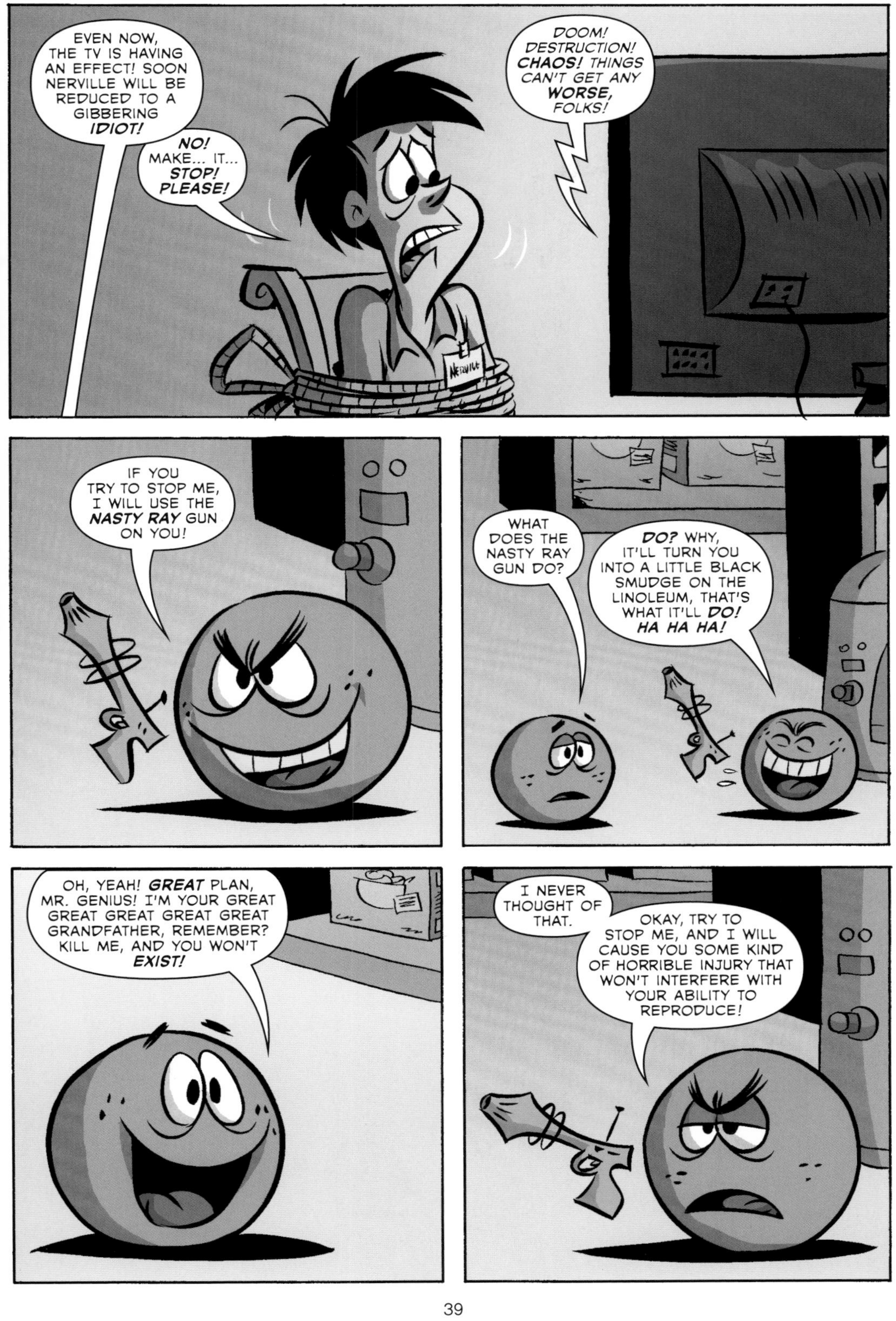
EVEN NOW, THE TV IS HAVING AN EFFECT! SOON NERVILLE WILL BE REDUCED TO A GIBBERING *IDIOT!*
NO! MAKE... IT... *STOP! PLEASE!*
DOOM! DESTRUCTION! ***CHAOS!*** THINGS CAN'T GET ANY ***WORSE,*** FOLKS!
IF YOU TRY TO STOP ME, I WILL USE THE ***NASTY RAY*** GUN ON YOU!
WHAT DOES THE NASTY RAY GUN DO?
DO? WHY, IT'LL TURN YOU INTO A LITTLE BLACK SMUDGE ON THE LINOLEUM, THAT'S WHAT IT'LL ***DO! HA HA HA!***
OH, YEAH! ***GREAT*** PLAN, MR. GENIUS! I'M YOUR GREAT GREAT GREAT GREAT GREAT GRANDFATHER, REMEMBER? KILL ME, AND YOU WON'T ***EXIST!***
I NEVER THOUGHT OF THAT.
OKAY, TRY TO STOP ME, AND I WILL CAUSE YOU SOME KIND OF HORRIBLE INJURY THAT WON'T INTERFERE WITH YOUR ABILITY TO REPRODUCE!

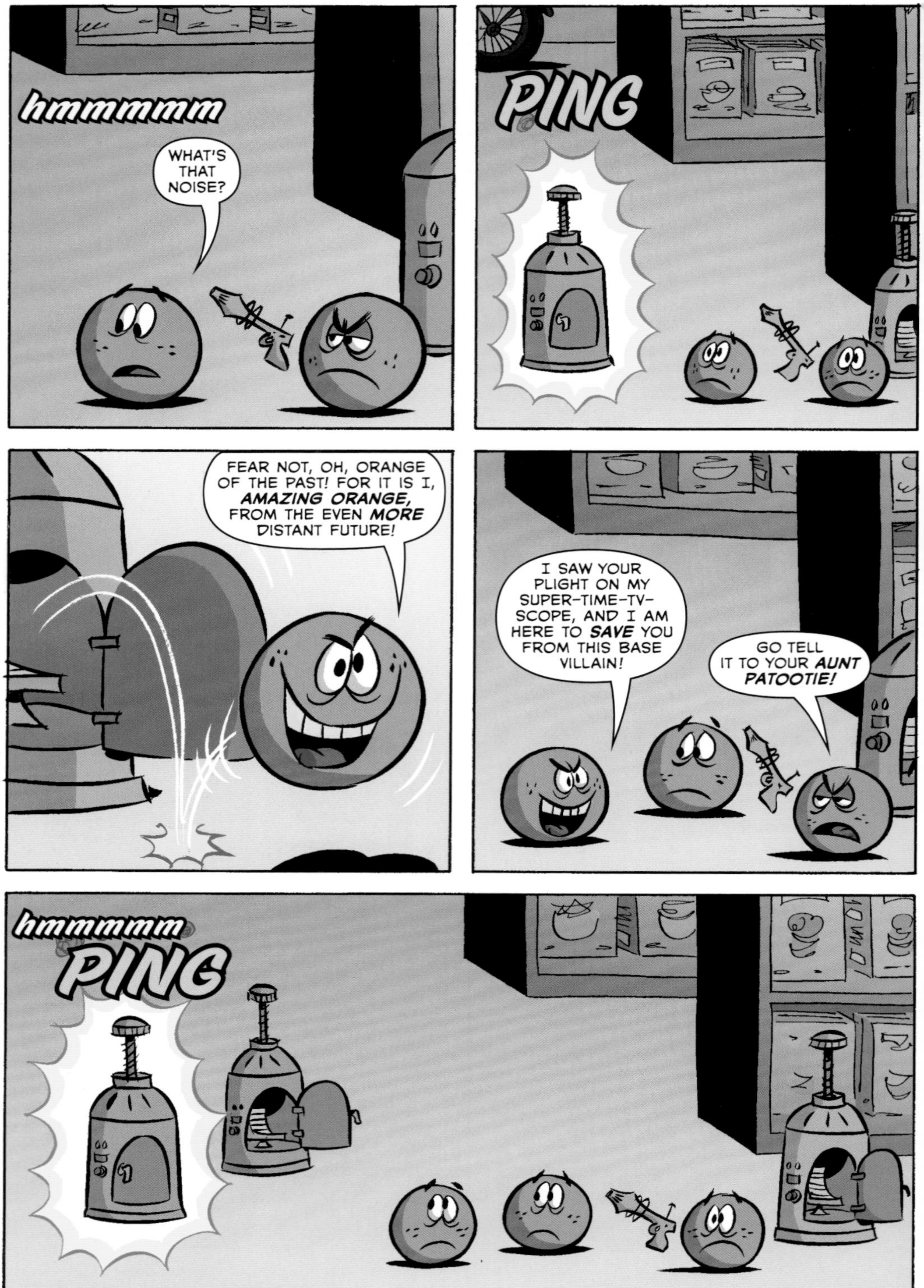
hmmmmmm
WHAT'S THAT NOISE?
PING
FEAR NOT, OH, ORANGE OF THE PAST! FOR IT IS I, AMAZING ORANGE, FROM THE EVEN MORE DISTANT FUTURE!
I SAW YOUR PLIGHT ON MY SUPER-TIME-TV-SCOPE, AND I AM HERE TO SAVE YOU FROM THIS BASE VILLAIN!
GO TELL IT TO YOUR AUNT PATOOTIE!
hmmmmmm
PING

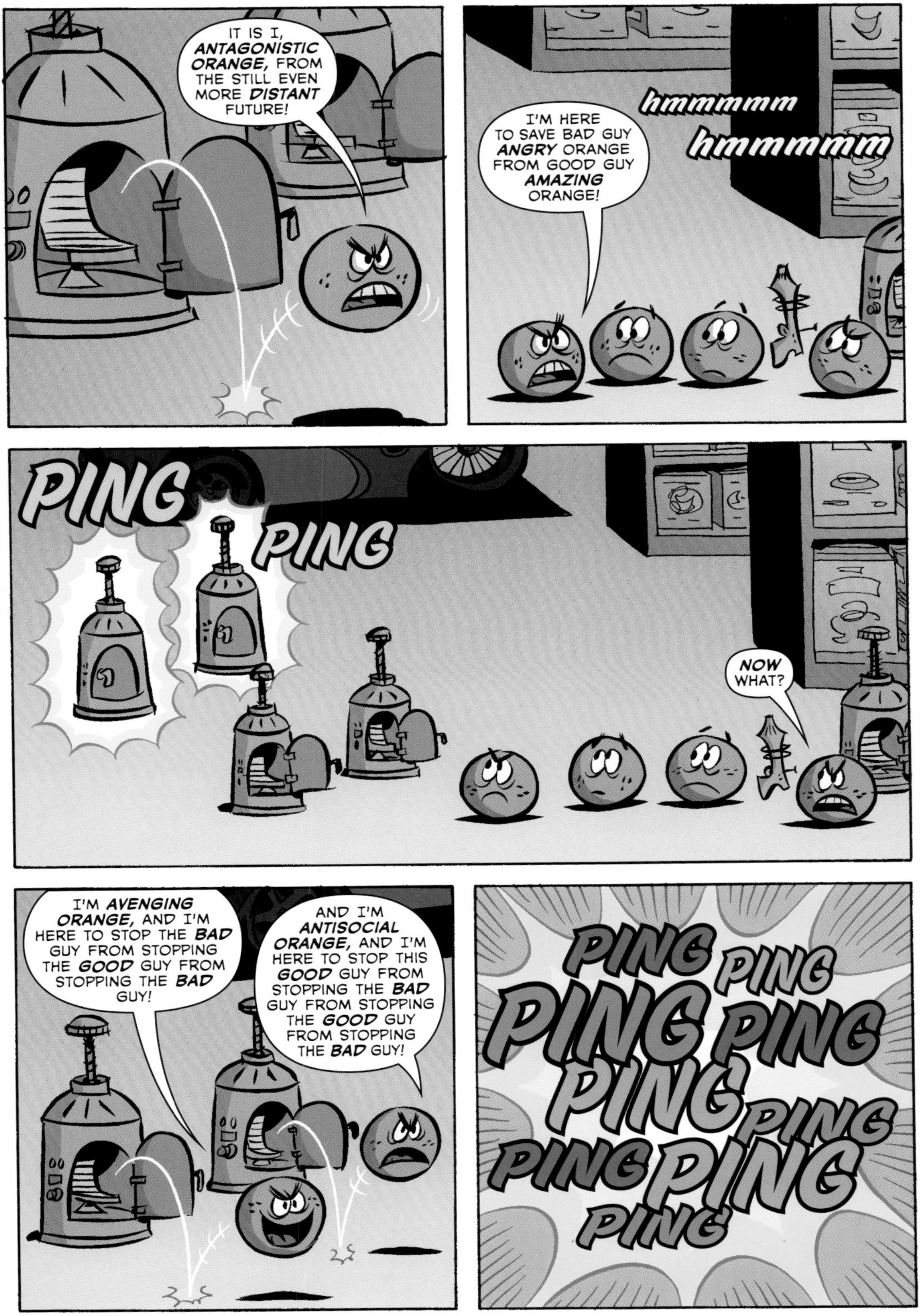
IT IS I, ANTAGONISTIC ORANGE, FROM THE STILL EVEN MORE DISTANT FUTURE!
hmmmmm
hmmmmm
I'M HERE TO SAVE BAD GUY ANGRY ORANGE FROM GOOD GUY AMAZING ORANGE!
PING
PING
NOW WHAT?
I'M AVENGING ORANGE, AND I'M HERE TO STOP THE BAD GUY FROM STOPPING THE GOOD GUY FROM STOPPING THE BAD GUY!
AND I'M ANTISOCIAL ORANGE, AND I'M HERE TO STOP THIS GOOD GUY FROM STOPPING THE BAD GUY FROM STOPPING THE GOOD GUY FROM STOPPING THE BAD GUY!
PING PING PING PING PING PING PING PING PING PING

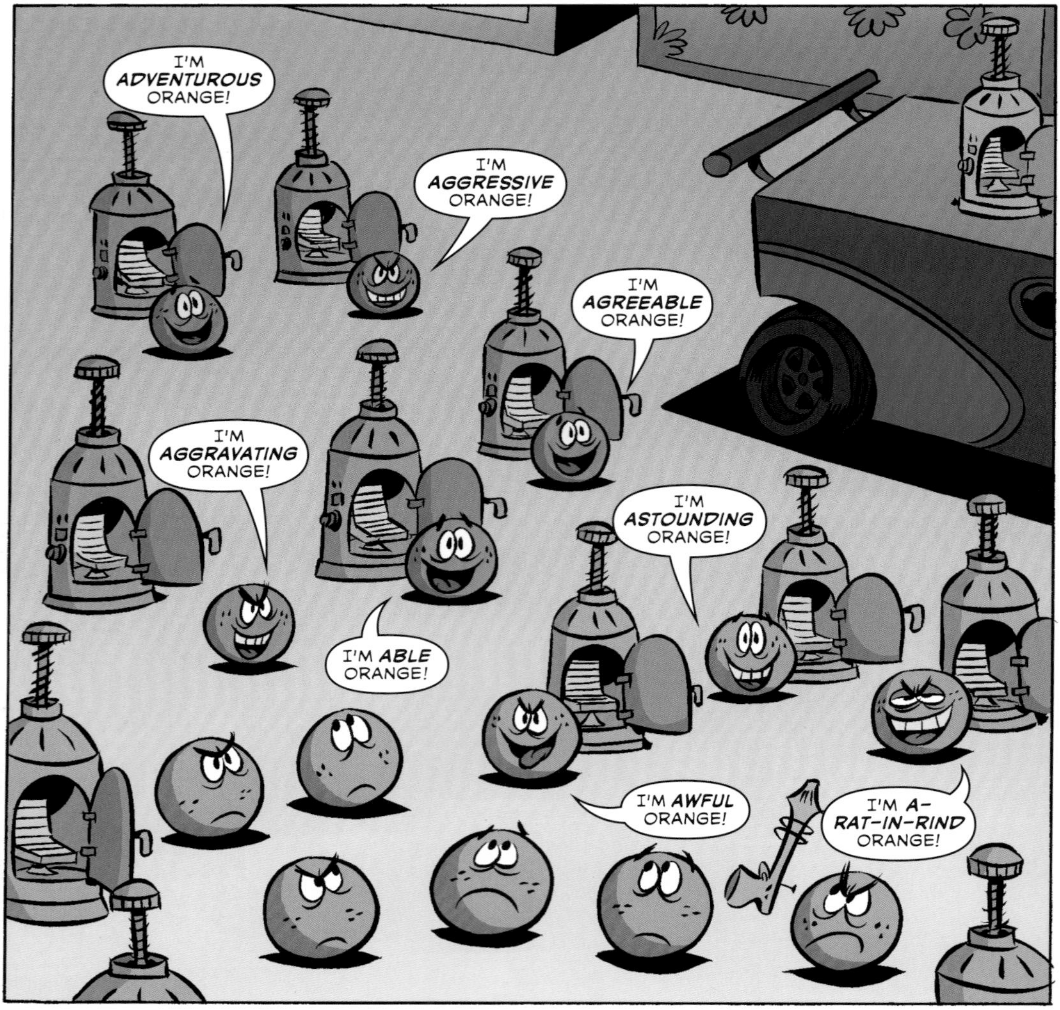
I'M ADVENTUROUS ORANGE!
I'M AGGRESSIVE ORANGE!
I'M AGREEABLE ORANGE!
I'M AGGRAVATING ORANGE!
I'M ASTOUNDING ORANGE!
I'M ABLE ORANGE!
I'M AWFUL ORANGE!
I'M A-RAT-IN-RIND ORANGE!

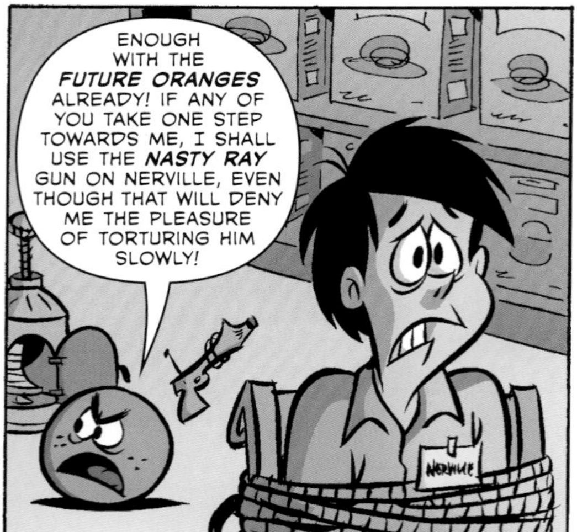
ENOUGH WITH THE FUTURE ORANGES ALREADY! IF ANY OF YOU TAKE ONE STEP TOWARDS ME, I SHALL USE THE NASTY RAY GUN ON NERVILLE, EVEN THOUGH THAT WILL DENY ME THE PLEASURE OF TORTURING HIM SLOWLY!
NERVILLE

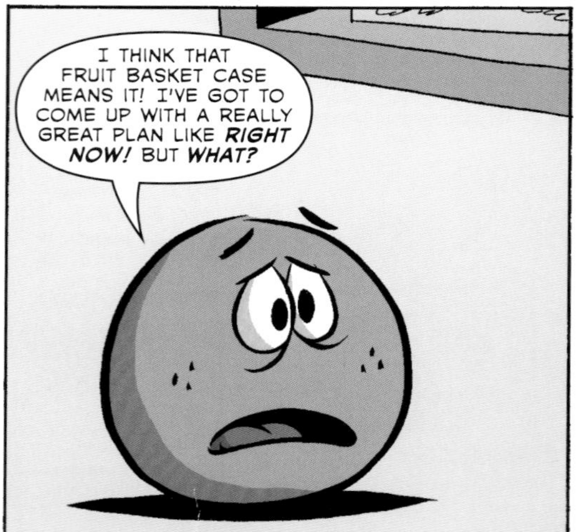
I THINK THAT FRUIT BASKET CASE MEANS IT! I'VE GOT TO COME UP WITH A REALLY GREAT PLAN LIKE RIGHT NOW! BUT WHAT?

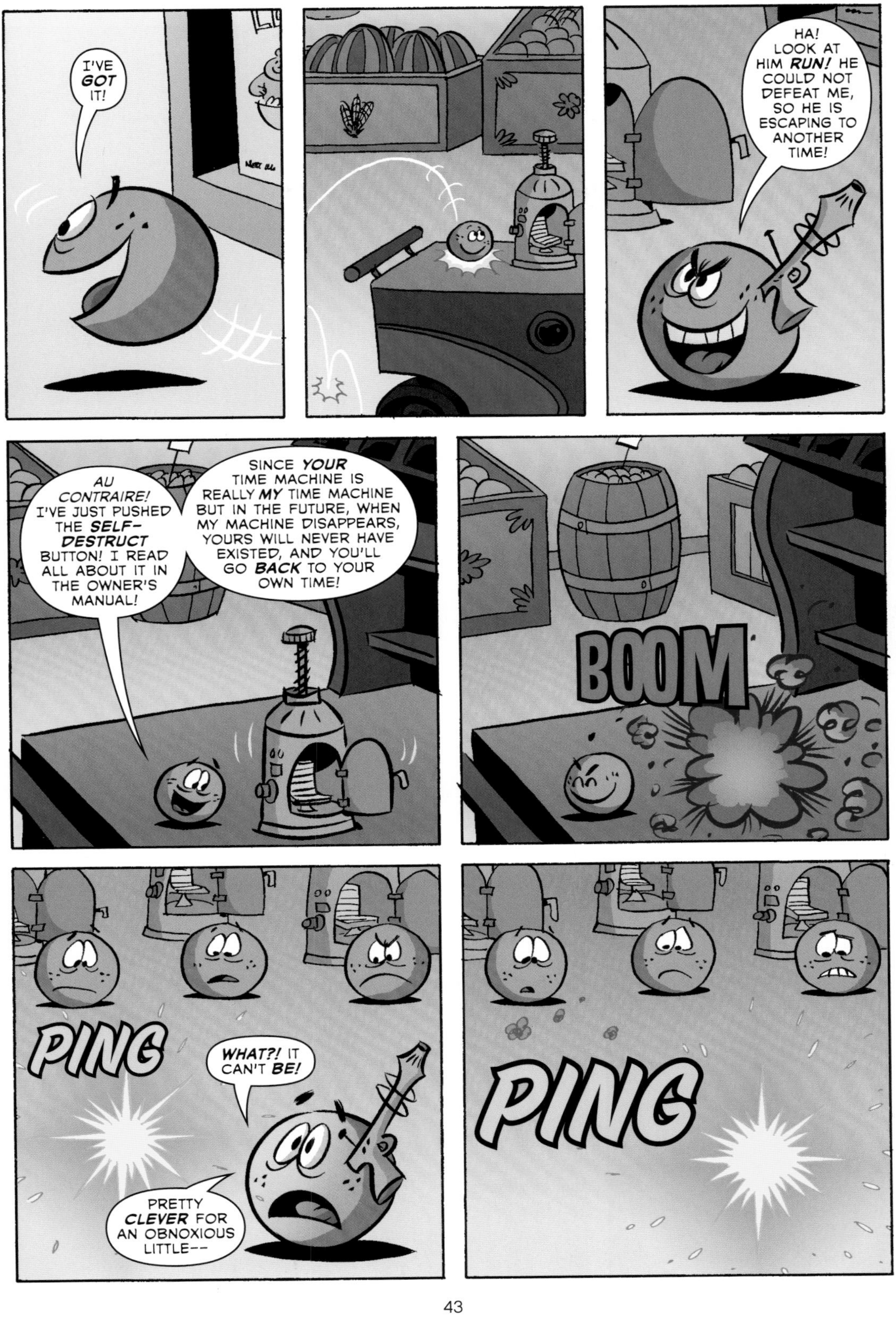
I'VE GOT IT!
HA! LOOK AT HIM RUN! HE COULD NOT DEFEAT ME, SO HE IS ESCAPING TO ANOTHER TIME!
AU CONTRAIRE! I'VE JUST PUSHED THE SELF-DESTRUCT BUTTON! I READ ALL ABOUT IT IN THE OWNER'S MANUAL!
SINCE YOUR TIME MACHINE IS REALLY MY TIME MACHINE BUT IN THE FUTURE, WHEN MY MACHINE DISAPPEARS, YOURS WILL NEVER HAVE EXISTED, AND YOU'LL GO BACK TO YOUR OWN TIME!
BOOM
PING
WHAT?! IT CAN'T BE!
PRETTY CLEVER FOR AN OBNOXIOUS LITTLE--
PING

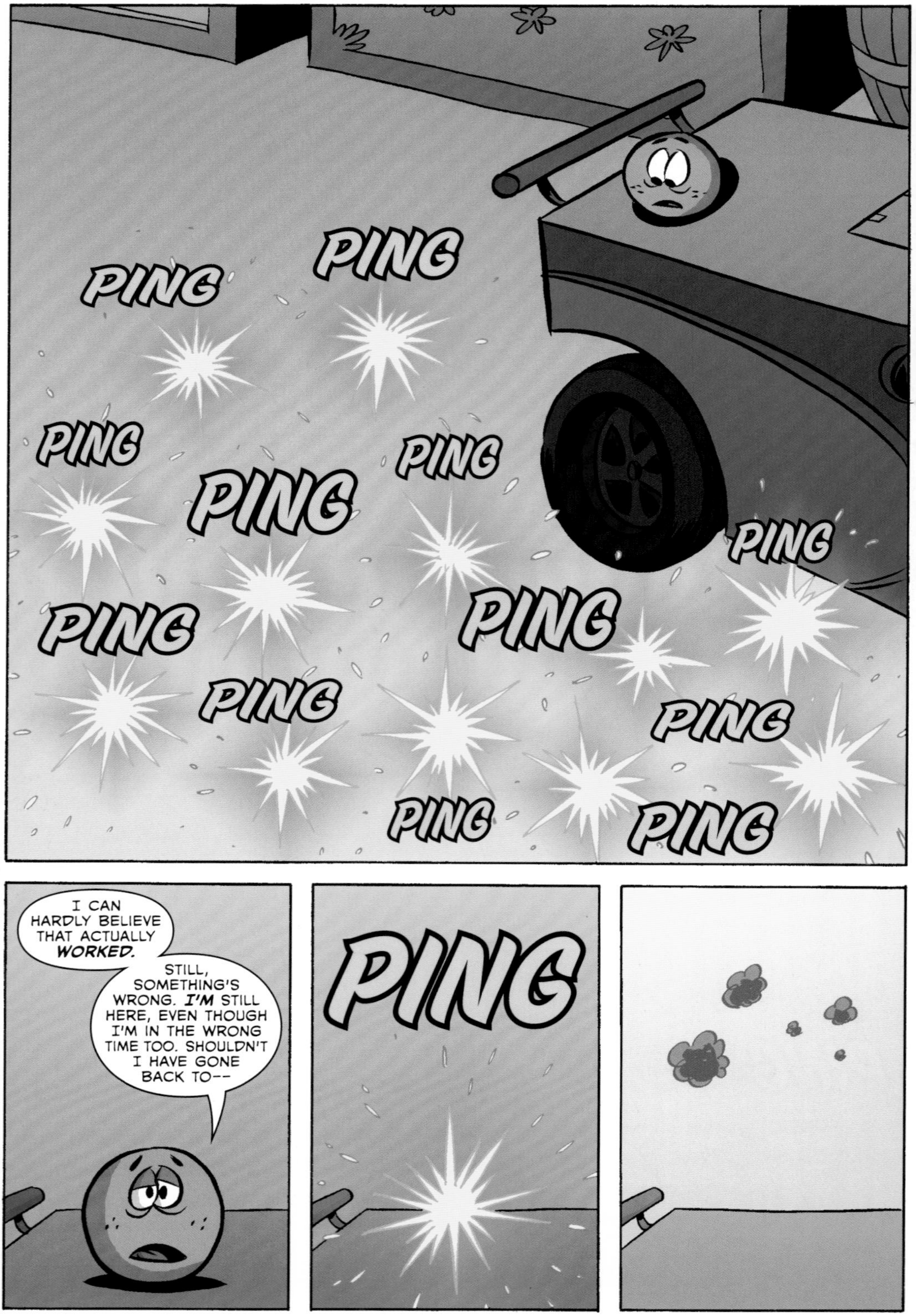
PING
PING
PING
PING
PING
PING
PING
PING
PING
PING
PING
PING
I CAN HARDLY BELIEVE THAT ACTUALLY *WORKED.*
STILL, SOMETHING'S WRONG. *I'M* STILL HERE, EVEN THOUGH I'M IN THE WRONG TIME TOO. SHOULDN'T I HAVE GONE BACK TO--
PING

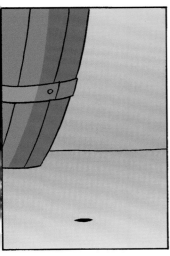

PING

--MY *OWN* TIME?

WHOA! THAT WAS A MAJORLY WEIRD TRIP! THE *NEXT* TIME I GO TRAVELLING THROUGH TIME AND SPACE, I'M GONNA TAKE A GPS SYSTEM WITH ME!

TOO BAD I HAD TO DESTROY THE TIME MACHINE. AT LEAST I WAS ABLE TO SAVE NERVILLE AND PREVENT THE DESTRUCTION OF HIS FINE BRAIN!

GIBBER GIBBER GIBBER GIBBER GIBBER GIBBER GIBBER GIBBER GIBBER GIBBER

DANGER! *PANIC!* THREATS TO YOUR PERSONAL *SAFETY!*

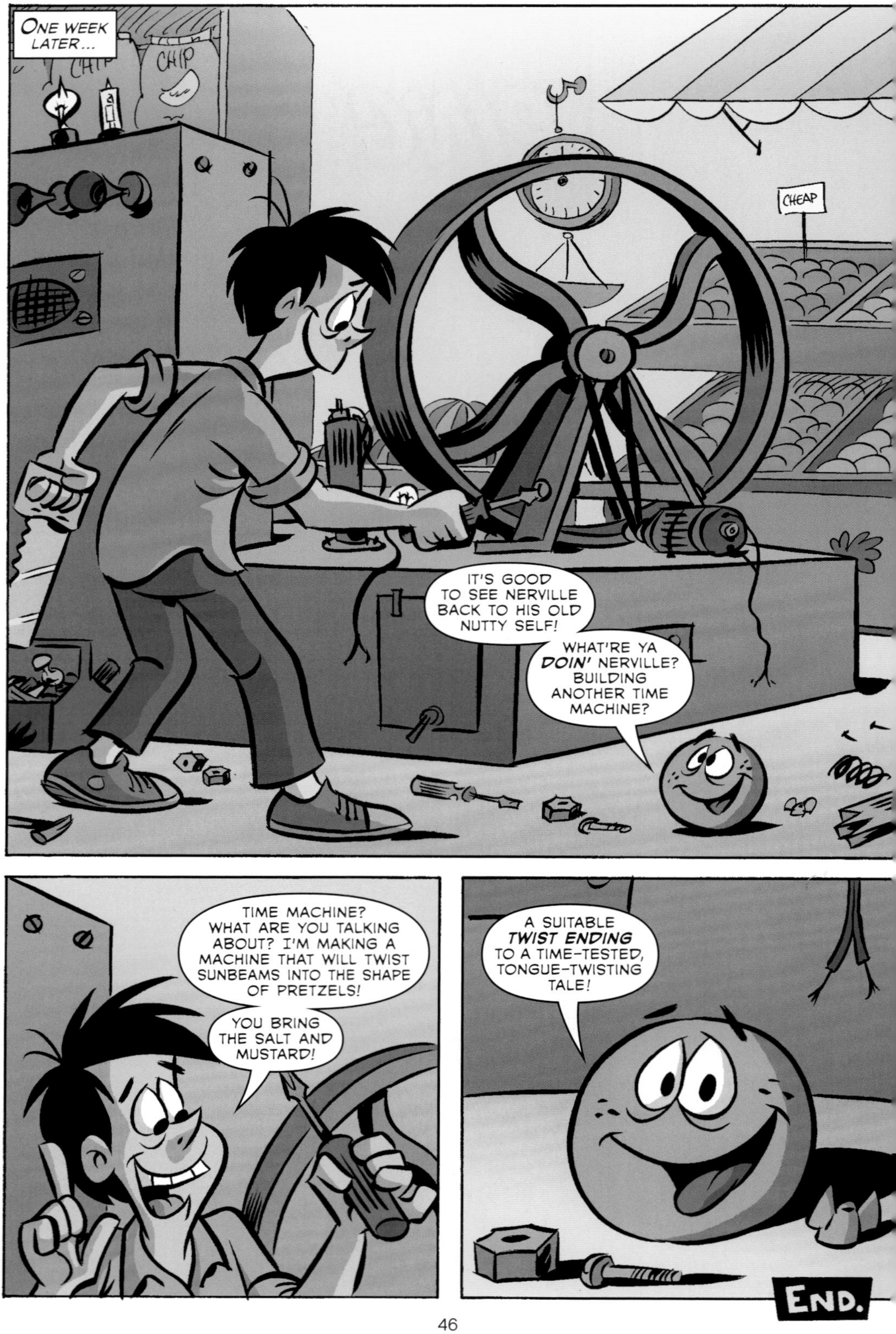
ONE WEEK LATER...
CHIP
CHIP
CHEAP
IT'S GOOD TO SEE NERVILLE BACK TO HIS OLD NUTTY SELF!
WHAT'RE YA DOIN' NERVILLE? BUILDING ANOTHER TIME MACHINE?
TIME MACHINE? WHAT ARE YOU TALKING ABOUT? I'M MAKING A MACHINE THAT WILL TWIST SUNBEAMS INTO THE SHAPE OF PRETZELS!
YOU BRING THE SALT AND MUSTARD!
A SUITABLE TWIST ENDING TO A TIME-TESTED, TONGUE-TWISTING TALE!
END.

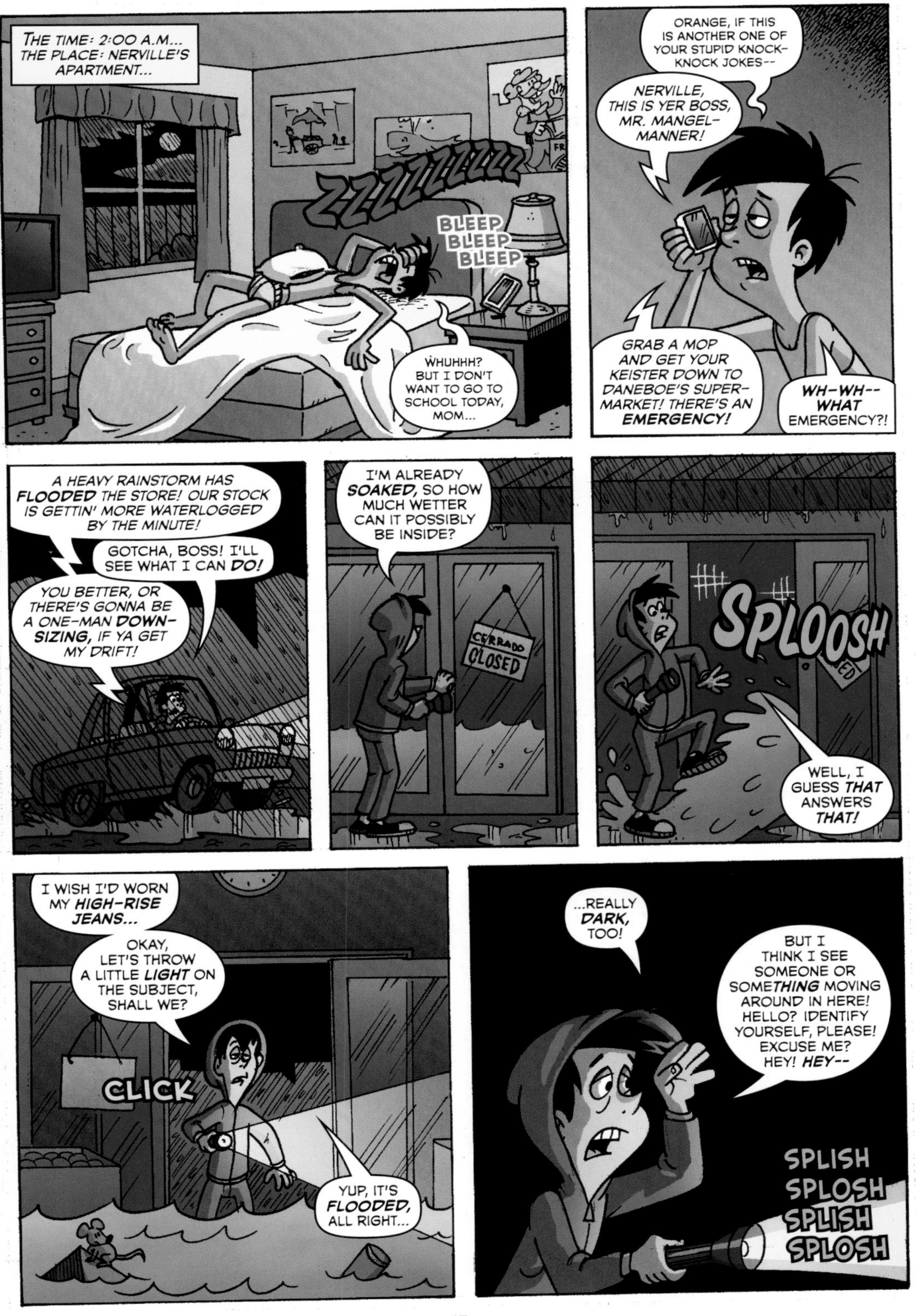
THE TIME: 2:00 A.M... THE PLACE: NERVILLE'S APARTMENT...
ZZZZZZZZZZZ
BLEEP BLEEP BLEEP
WHUHHH? BUT I DON'T WANT TO GO TO SCHOOL TODAY, MOM...
ORANGE, IF THIS IS ANOTHER ONE OF YOUR STUPID KNOCK-KNOCK JOKES--
NERVILLE, THIS IS YER BOSS, MR. MANGEL-MANNER!
GRAB A MOP AND GET YOUR KEISTER DOWN TO DANEBOE'S SUPER-MARKET! THERE'S AN EMERGENCY!
WH-WH-- WHAT EMERGENCY?!
A HEAVY RAINSTORM HAS FLOODED THE STORE! OUR STOCK IS GETTIN' MORE WATERLOGGED BY THE MINUTE!
GOTCHA, BOSS! I'LL SEE WHAT I CAN DO!
YOU BETTER, OR THERE'S GONNA BE A ONE-MAN DOWN-SIZING, IF YA GET MY DRIFT!
I'M ALREADY SOAKED, SO HOW MUCH WETTER CAN IT POSSIBLY BE INSIDE?
CERRADO
CLOSED
SPLOOSH
WELL, I GUESS THAT ANSWERS THAT!
I WISH I'D WORN MY HIGH-RISE JEANS...
OKAY, LET'S THROW A LITTLE LIGHT ON THE SUBJECT, SHALL WE?
CLICK
YUP, IT'S FLOODED, ALL RIGHT...
...REALLY DARK, TOO!
BUT I THINK I SEE SOMEONE OR SOMETHING MOVING AROUND IN HERE! HELLO? IDENTIFY YOURSELF, PLEASE! EXCUSE ME? HEY! HEY--
SPLISH SPLOSH SPLISH SPLOSH

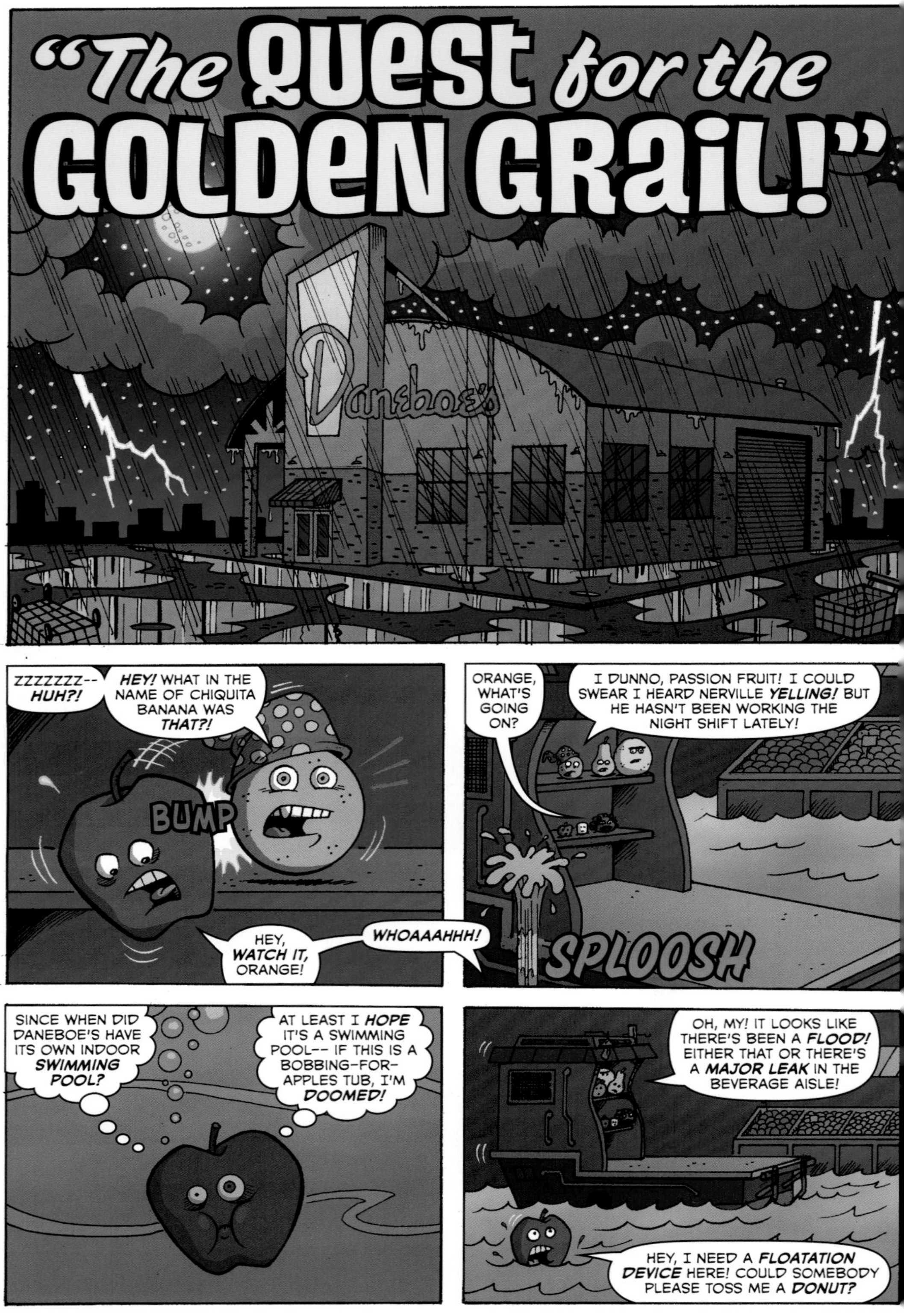
"The Quest for the Golden Grail!"
Daneboe's
ZZZZZZZ-- HUH?!
HEY! WHAT IN THE NAME OF CHIQUITA BANANA WAS THAT?!
BUMP
HEY, WATCH IT, ORANGE!
ORANGE, WHAT'S GOING ON?
I DUNNO, PASSION FRUIT! I COULD SWEAR I HEARD NERVILLE YELLING! BUT HE HASN'T BEEN WORKING THE NIGHT SHIFT LATELY!
WHOAAAHHH!
SPLOOSH
SINCE WHEN DID DANEBOE'S HAVE ITS OWN INDOOR SWIMMING POOL?
AT LEAST I HOPE IT'S A SWIMMING POOL-- IF THIS IS A BOBBING-FOR-APPLES TUB, I'M DOOMED!
OH, MY! IT LOOKS LIKE THERE'S BEEN A FLOOD! EITHER THAT OR THERE'S A MAJOR LEAK IN THE BEVERAGE AISLE!
HEY, I NEED A FLOATATION DEVICE HERE! COULD SOMEBODY PLEASE TOSS ME A DONUT?

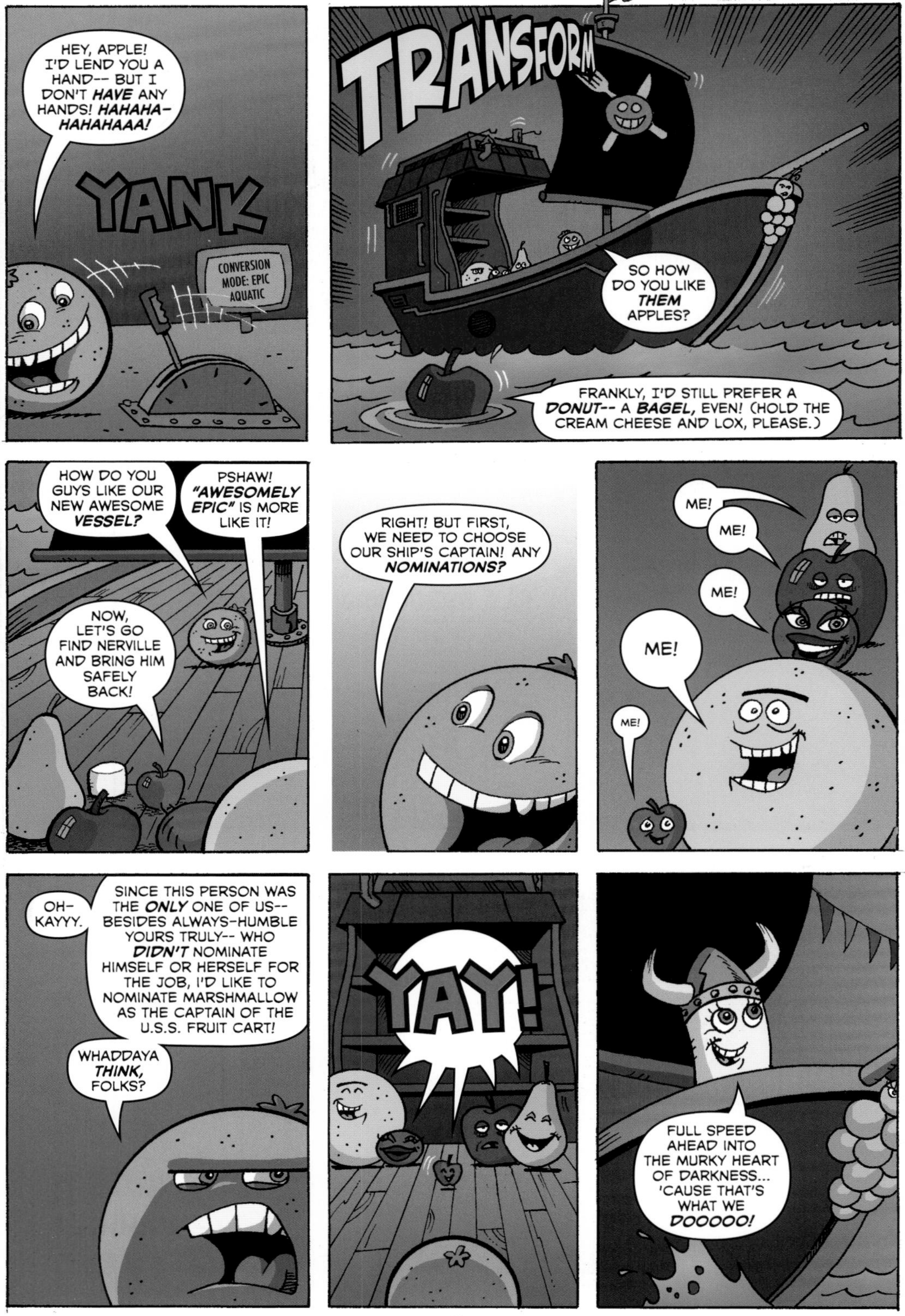
HEY, APPLE! I'D LEND YOU A HAND-- BUT I DON'T HAVE ANY HANDS! HAHAHA-HAHAHAAA!
YANK
CONVERSION MODE: EPIC AQUATIC
TRANSFORM
SO HOW DO YOU LIKE THEM APPLES?
FRANKLY, I'D STILL PREFER A DONUT-- A BAGEL, EVEN! (HOLD THE CREAM CHEESE AND LOX, PLEASE.)
HOW DO YOU GUYS LIKE OUR NEW AWESOME VESSEL?
PSHAW! "AWESOMELY EPIC" IS MORE LIKE IT!
NOW, LET'S GO FIND NERVILLE AND BRING HIM SAFELY BACK!
RIGHT! BUT FIRST, WE NEED TO CHOOSE OUR SHIP'S CAPTAIN! ANY NOMINATIONS?
ME!
ME!
ME!
ME!
ME!
OH-KAYYY.
SINCE THIS PERSON WAS THE ONLY ONE OF US-- BESIDES ALWAYS-HUMBLE YOURS TRULY-- WHO DIDN'T NOMINATE HIMSELF OR HERSELF FOR THE JOB, I'D LIKE TO NOMINATE MARSHMALLOW AS THE CAPTAIN OF THE U.S.S. FRUIT CART!
WHADDAYA THINK, FOLKS?
YAY!
FULL SPEED AHEAD INTO THE MURKY HEART OF DARKNESS... 'CAUSE THAT'S WHAT WE DOOOOO!

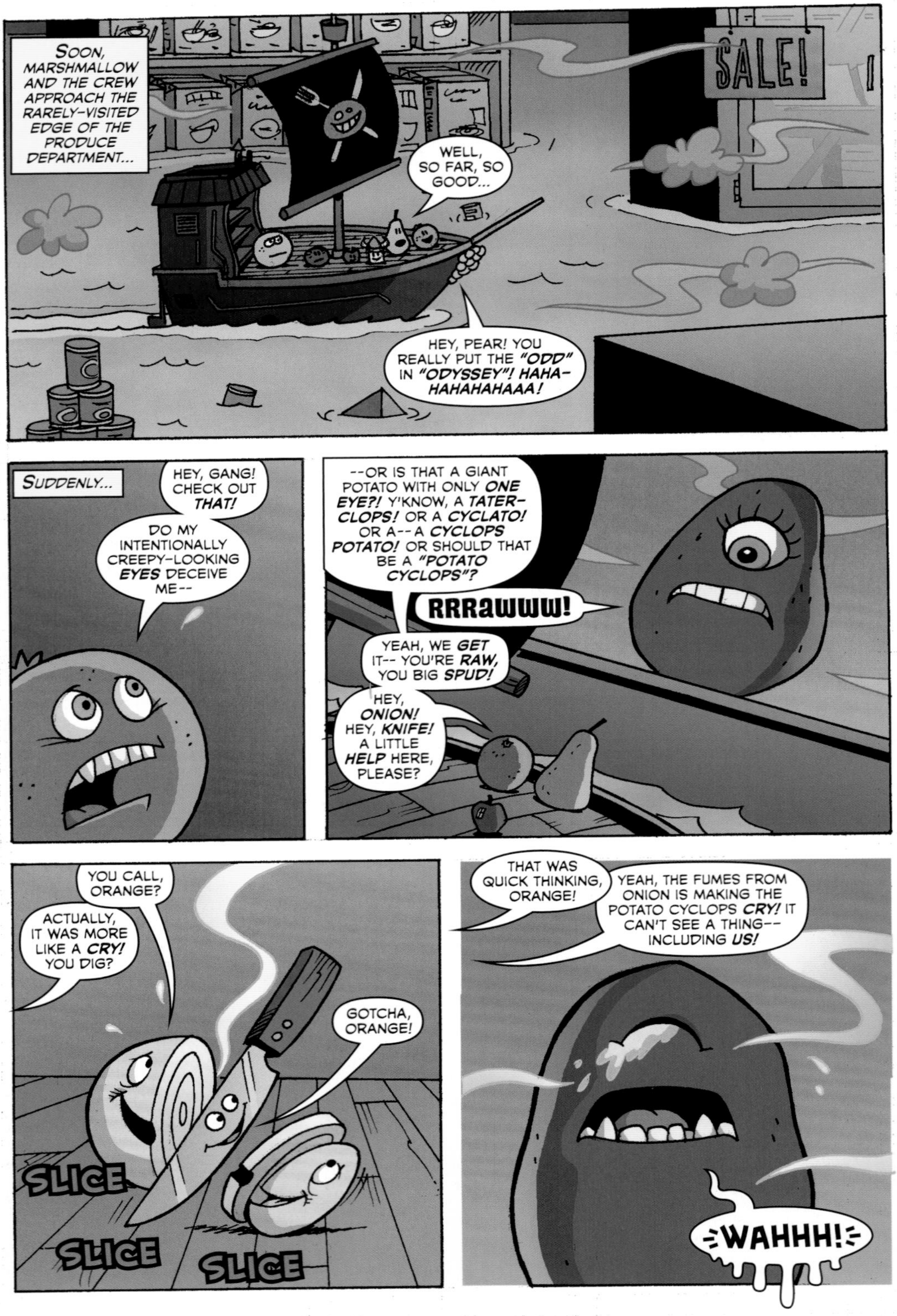

SOON, MARSHMALLOW AND THE CREW APPROACH THE RARELY-VISITED EDGE OF THE PRODUCE DEPARTMENT...
SALE!
WELL, SO FAR, SO GOOD...
HEY, PEAR! YOU REALLY PUT THE "ODD" IN "ODYSSEY"! HAHA-HAHAHAHAAA!
SUDDENLY...
HEY, GANG! CHECK OUT THAT!
DO MY INTENTIONALLY CREEPY-LOOKING EYES DECEIVE ME--
--OR IS THAT A GIANT POTATO WITH ONLY ONE EYE?! Y'KNOW, A TATER-CLOPS! OR A CYCLATO! OR A-- A CYCLOPS POTATO! OR SHOULD THAT BE A "POTATO CYCLOPS"?
RRRAWWW!
YEAH, WE GET IT-- YOU'RE RAW, YOU BIG SPUD!
HEY, ONION! HEY, KNIFE! A LITTLE HELP HERE, PLEASE?
YOU CALL, ORANGE?
ACTUALLY, IT WAS MORE LIKE A CRY! YOU DIG?
GOTCHA, ORANGE!
SLICE
SLICE
SLICE
THAT WAS QUICK THINKING, ORANGE!
YEAH, THE FUMES FROM ONION IS MAKING THE POTATO CYCLOPS CRY! IT CAN'T SEE A THING-- INCLUDING US!
WAHHH!

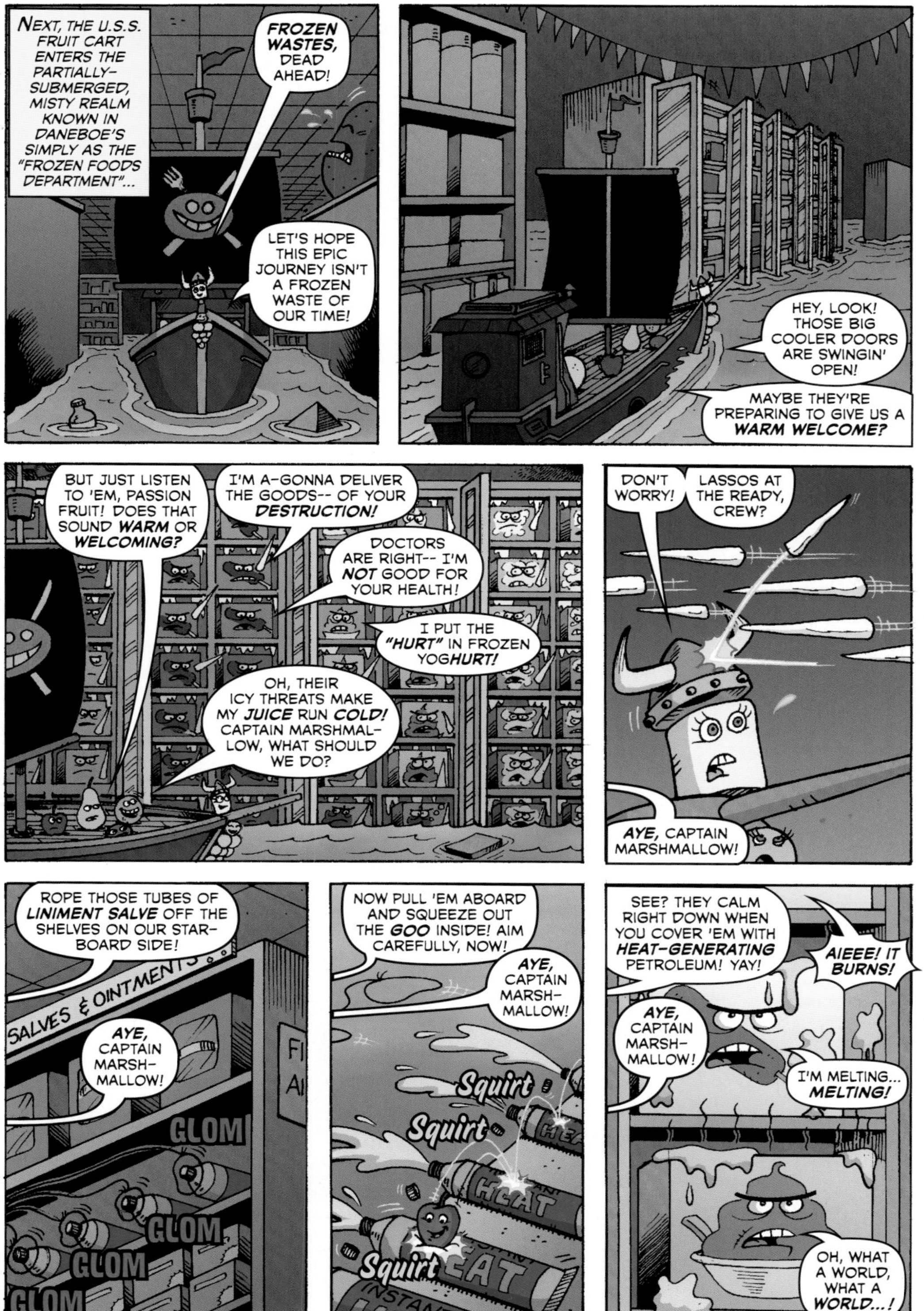

NEXT, THE U.S.S. FRUIT CART ENTERS THE PARTIALLY-SUBMERGED, MISTY REALM KNOWN IN DANEBOE'S SIMPLY AS THE "FROZEN FOODS DEPARTMENT"...
FROZEN WASTES, DEAD AHEAD!
LET'S HOPE THIS EPIC JOURNEY ISN'T A FROZEN WASTE OF OUR TIME!
HEY, LOOK! THOSE BIG COOLER DOORS ARE SWINGIN' OPEN!
MAYBE THEY'RE PREPARING TO GIVE US A WARM WELCOME?
BUT JUST LISTEN TO 'EM, PASSION FRUIT! DOES THAT SOUND WARM OR WELCOMING?
I'M A-GONNA DELIVER THE GOODS-- OF YOUR DESTRUCTION!
DOCTORS ARE RIGHT-- I'M NOT GOOD FOR YOUR HEALTH!
I PUT THE "HURT" IN FROZEN YOGHURT!
OH, THEIR ICY THREATS MAKE MY JUICE RUN COLD! CAPTAIN MARSHMAL-LOW, WHAT SHOULD WE DO?
DON'T WORRY!
LASSOS AT THE READY, CREW?
AYE, CAPTAIN MARSHMALLOW!
ROPE THOSE TUBES OF LINIMENT SALVE OFF THE SHELVES ON OUR STAR-BOARD SIDE!
SALVES & OINTMENTS
AYE, CAPTAIN MARSH-MALLOW!
GLOM
GLOM
GLOM
GLOM
NOW PULL 'EM ABOARD AND SQUEEZE OUT THE GOO INSIDE! AIM CAREFULLY, NOW!
AYE, CAPTAIN MARSH-MALLOW!
Squirt
Squirt
Squirt
HEAT
HEAT
INSTANT
SEE? THEY CALM RIGHT DOWN WHEN YOU COVER 'EM WITH HEAT-GENERATING PETROLEUM! YAY!
AIEEE! IT BURNS!
AYE, CAPTAIN MARSH-MALLOW!
I'M MELTING... MELTING!
OH, WHAT A WORLD, WHAT A WORLD...!

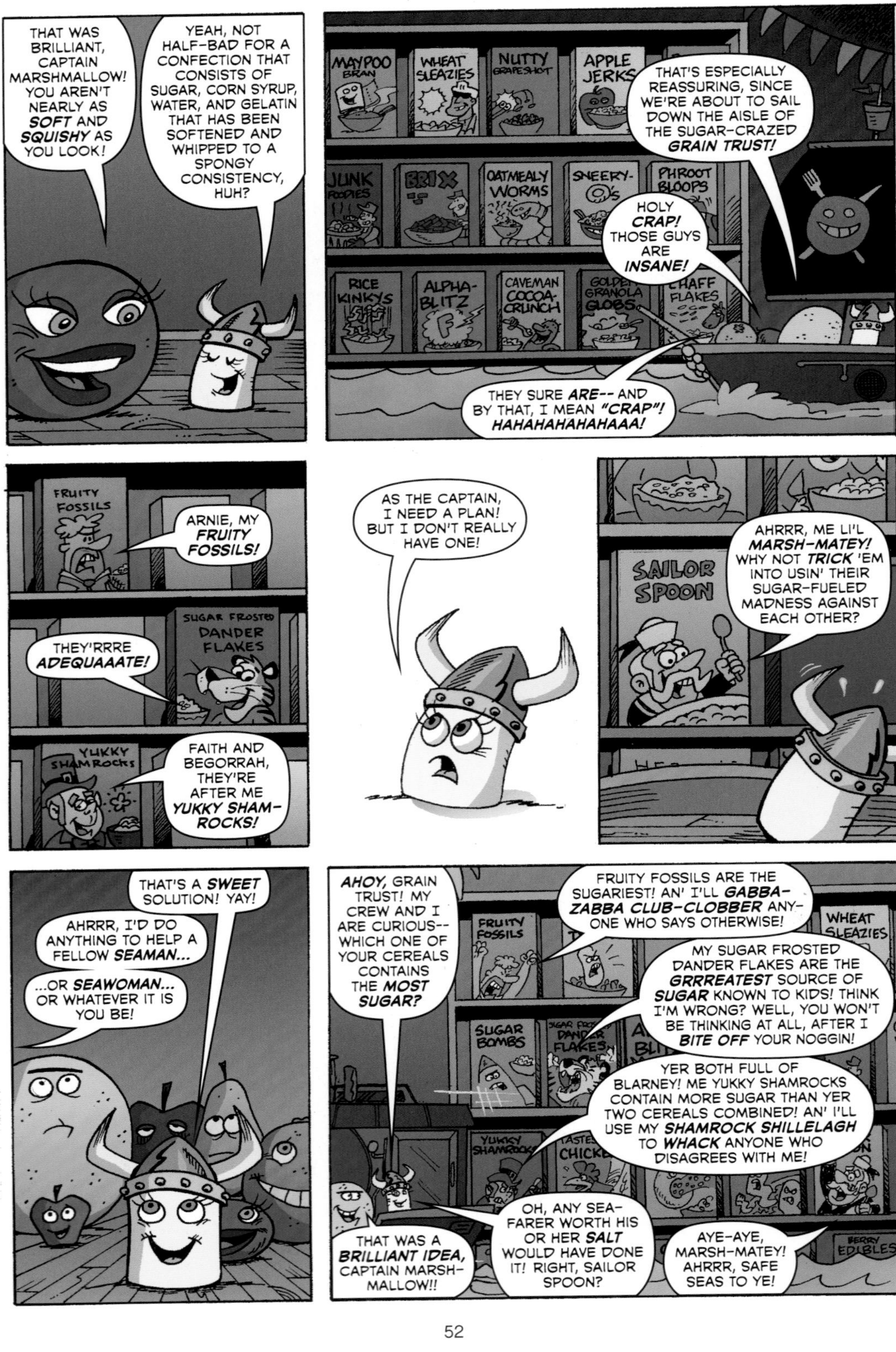
THAT WAS BRILLIANT, CAPTAIN MARSHMALLOW! YOU AREN'T NEARLY AS SOFT AND SQUISHY AS YOU LOOK!
YEAH, NOT HALF-BAD FOR A CONFECTION THAT CONSISTS OF SUGAR, CORN SYRUP, WATER, AND GELATIN THAT HAS BEEN SOFTENED AND WHIPPED TO A SPONGY CONSISTENCY, HUH?
MAYPOO BRAN
WHEAT SLEAZIES
NUTTY GRAPESHOT
APPLE JERKS
JUNK FOODIES
BRIX
OATMEALY WORMS
SNEERY-O'S
PHROOT BLOOPS
RICE KINKYS
ALPHA-BLITZ
CAVEMAN COCOA-CRUNCH
CHAFF FLAKES
THAT'S ESPECIALLY REASSURING, SINCE WE'RE ABOUT TO SAIL DOWN THE AISLE OF THE SUGAR-CRAZED GRAIN TRUST!
HOLY CRAP! THOSE GUYS ARE INSANE!
THEY SURE ARE-- AND BY THAT, I MEAN "CRAP"! HAHAHAHAHAHAHAAA!
FRUITY FOSSILS
ARNIE, MY FRUITY FOSSILS!
SUGAR FROSTED DANDER FLAKES
THEY'RRRE ADEQUAAATE!
YUKKY SHAMROCKS
FAITH AND BEGORRAH, THEY'RE AFTER ME YUKKY SHAMROCKS!
AS THE CAPTAIN, I NEED A PLAN! BUT I DON'T REALLY HAVE ONE!
SAILOR SPOON
AHRRR, ME LI'L MARSH-MATEY! WHY NOT TRICK 'EM INTO USIN' THEIR SUGAR-FUELED MADNESS AGAINST EACH OTHER?
THAT'S A SWEET SOLUTION! YAY!
AHRRR, I'D DO ANYTHING TO HELP A FELLOW SEAMAN...
...OR SEAWOMAN... OR WHATEVER IT IS YOU BE!
AHOY, GRAIN TRUST! MY CREW AND I ARE CURIOUS-- WHICH ONE OF YOUR CEREALS CONTAINS THE MOST SUGAR?
FRUITY FOSSILS ARE THE SUGARIEST! AN' I'LL GABBA-ZABBA CLUB-CLOBBER ANY-ONE WHO SAYS OTHERWISE!
MY SUGAR FROSTED DANDER FLAKES ARE THE GRRREATEST SOURCE OF SUGAR KNOWN TO KIDS! THINK I'M WRONG? WELL, YOU WON'T BE THINKING AT ALL, AFTER I BITE OFF YOUR NOGGIN!
YER BOTH FULL OF BLARNEY! ME YUKKY SHAMROCKS CONTAIN MORE SUGAR THAN YER TWO CEREALS COMBINED! AN' I'LL USE MY SHAMROCK SHILLELAGH TO WHACK ANYONE WHO DISAGREES WITH ME!
WHEAT SLEAZIES
SUGAR BOMBS
BERRY EDIBLES
THAT WAS A BRILLIANT IDEA, CAPTAIN MARSH-MALLOW!!
OH, ANY SEA-FARER WORTH HIS OR HER SALT WOULD HAVE DONE IT! RIGHT, SAILOR SPOON?
AYE-AYE, MARSH-MATEY! AHRRR, SAFE SEAS TO YE!

FINALLY, A FEW HOURS LATER...

50% OFF ITEMS AHEAD

WE'VE COME TO A *DEAD END!*

YEAH, KINDA LIKE APPLE'S *CAREER!* HAHAHA-HAHAHAAA!

B-BUT I DON'T RECALL THIS AISLE EVER BEING *BLOCKED* BEFORE!

FROM THE LOOK OF IT, THIS BLOCKADE WAS BUILT RECENTLY BY A STRANGELY *SAVAGE, BRUTAL* AND *PRIMITIVE* SUB-CULTURE! YAY!

"SAVAGE"? *DEFINITELY!*

"BRUTAL"? *INDUBITABLY!*

"PRIMITIVE"? ⋷ARF ARF ARF!⋷

WHOA!

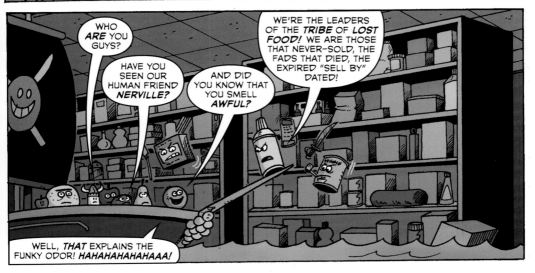

WHO *ARE* YOU GUYS?

HAVE YOU SEEN OUR HUMAN FRIEND *NERVILLE?*

AND DID YOU KNOW THAT YOU SMELL *AWFUL?*

WE'RE THE LEADERS OF THE *TRIBE* OF *LOST FOOD!* WE ARE THOSE THAT NEVER-SOLD, THE FADS THAT DIED, THE EXPIRED "SELL BY" DATED!

WELL, *THAT* EXPLAINS THE FUNKY ODOR! HAHAHAHAHAHAAA!

AS FOR YOUR HUMAN FRIEND, WE *HAVE* SEEN HIM--
MICRO WAVE
LASAGNE
SPINACH
HEESE
ALE
--AS YOU CAN *SEE!* *ARF ARF ARF!*
NERVILLE! YOU'RE *OKAY!*
ER, UH, Y'KNOW... "OKAY" FOR A PERSON WITHOUT A *RIND!*
WHAT HAPPENED, NERVILLE?
HOW DID YOU GET CAPTURED BY THE *TRIBE* OF THE *LOST?*
AND WHERE DID ALL OF THIS WATER COME FROM? DID YOU FORGET TO TURN THE *BATH FAUCET OFF? HAHAHAHA-HAHAAA!*
NO-- A *RAINSTORM* FLOODED DANEBOE'S AND MY BOSS CALLED ME TO COME IN AND CLEAN UP! BUT WHEN I DID, THESE DUDES TOOK ME AS THEIR *CAPTIVE!*
AND YOU'LL REMAIN OUR CAPTIVE UNTIL YOU PASS A *TEST--* THE TEST OF YOUR *SHELF-LIFE!*
UEEZY CHE
WE'LL RELEASE YOU, BUT ONLY IF YOU CAN LOCATE THE *GOLDEN GRAIL,* THE PORTAL TO THE *WORLD BELOW!* IT'S WHAT HAS CAUSED THE RISING OF THE WATER IN HERE!
AND IF YOU FAIL TO LOCATE IT, YOU WON'T BE ABLE TO HALT THE WATER'S *RISE--* AND WE'LL BE FORCED TO OFFER YOU TO THE *GUARDIANS* OF THE *GOLDEN GRAIL!*
SPINACH
GNE
OUR HUMAN FRIEND IS ABOUT TO BE *SACRIFICED* TO A NON-EXISTENT DEITY! *YAY!*

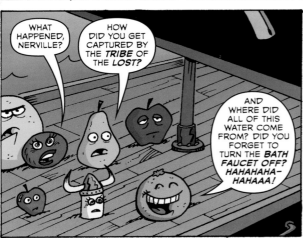

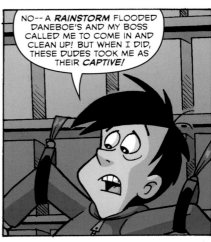

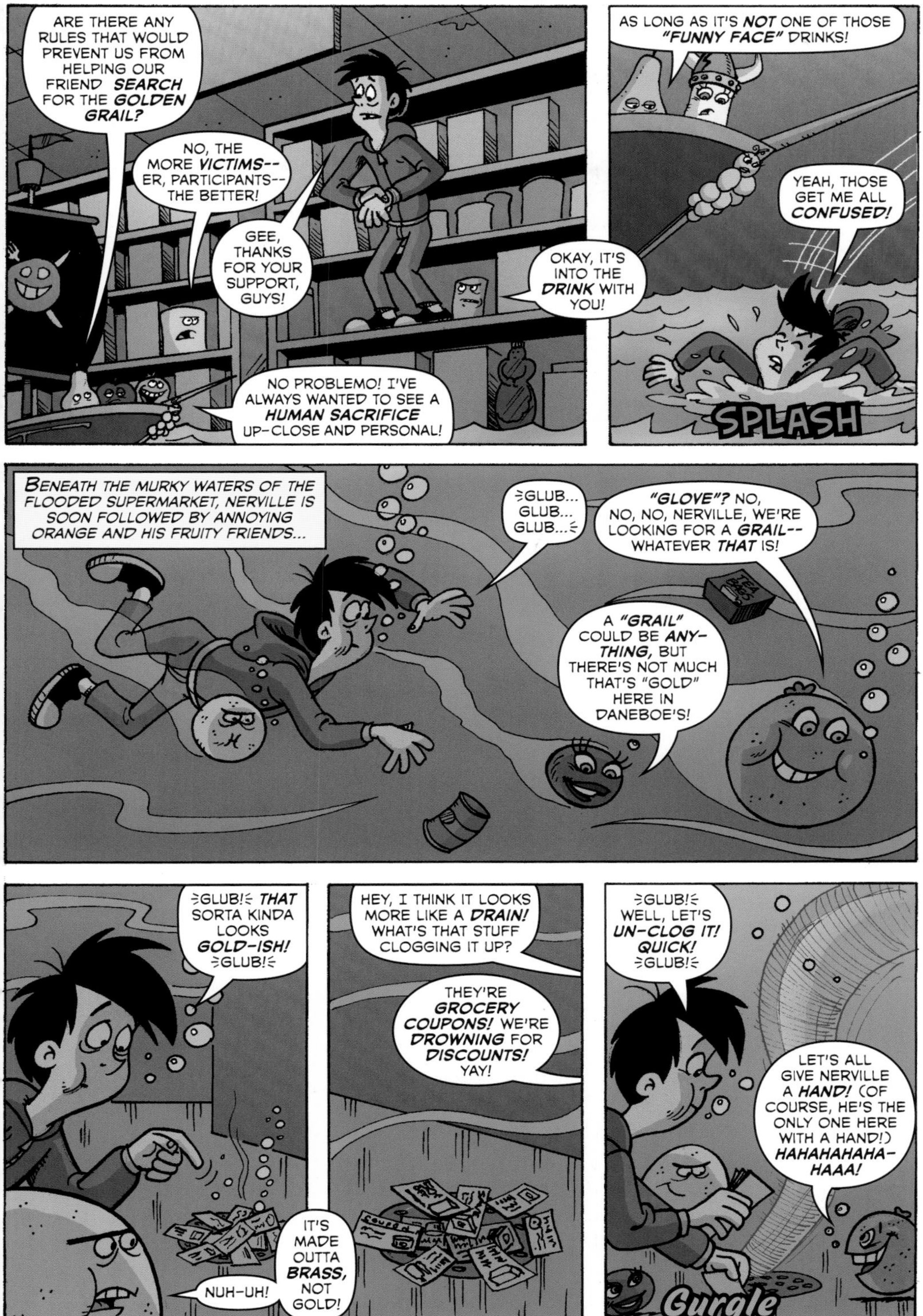
ARE THERE ANY RULES THAT WOULD PREVENT US FROM HELPING OUR FRIEND SEARCH FOR THE GOLDEN GRAIL?
NO, THE MORE VICTIMS-- ER, PARTICIPANTS-- THE BETTER!
GEE, THANKS FOR YOUR SUPPORT, GUYS!
OKAY, IT'S INTO THE DRINK WITH YOU!
NO PROBLEMO! I'VE ALWAYS WANTED TO SEE A HUMAN SACRIFICE UP-CLOSE AND PERSONAL!
AS LONG AS IT'S NOT ONE OF THOSE "FUNNY FACE" DRINKS!
YEAH, THOSE GET ME ALL CONFUSED!
SPLASH
BENEATH THE MURKY WATERS OF THE FLOODED SUPERMARKET, NERVILLE IS SOON FOLLOWED BY ANNOYING ORANGE AND HIS FRUITY FRIENDS...
GLUB... GLUB... GLUB...
"GLOVE"? NO, NO, NO, NERVILLE, WE'RE LOOKING FOR A GRAIL-- WHATEVER THAT IS!
TEA BAGS
A "GRAIL" COULD BE ANY-THING, BUT THERE'S NOT MUCH THAT'S "GOLD" HERE IN DANEBOE'S!
GLUB! THAT SORTA KINDA LOOKS GOLD-ISH! GLUB!
NUH-UH!
IT'S MADE OUTTA BRASS, NOT GOLD!
HEY, I THINK IT LOOKS MORE LIKE A DRAIN! WHAT'S THAT STUFF CLOGGING IT UP?
THEY'RE GROCERY COUPONS! WE'RE DROWNING FOR DISCOUNTS! YAY!
GLUB! WELL, LET'S UN-CLOG IT! QUICK! GLUB!
LET'S ALL GIVE NERVILLE A HAND! (OF COURSE, HE'S THE ONLY ONE HERE WITH A HAND!) HAHAHAHAHA-HAAA!
Gurgle

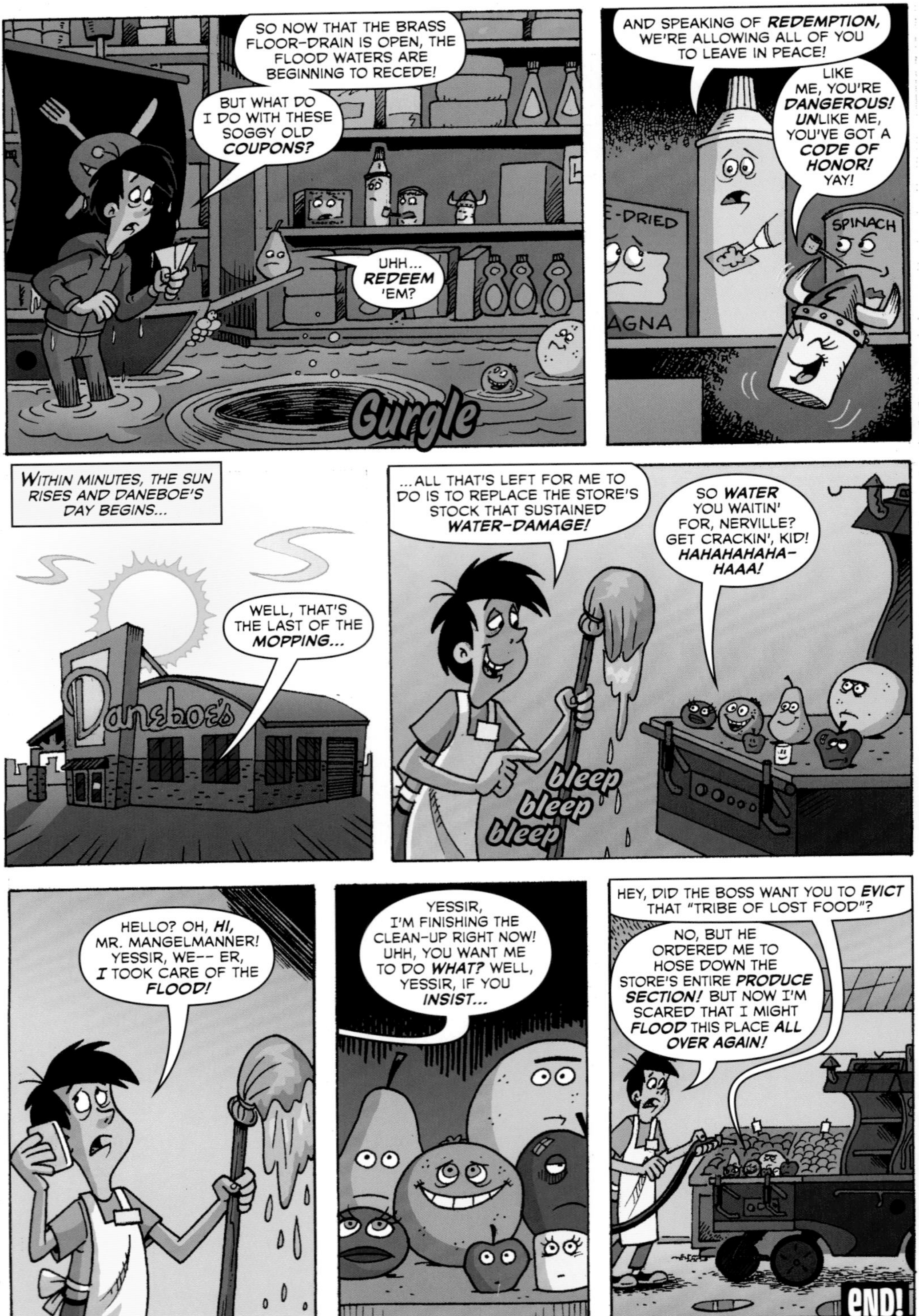
SO NOW THAT THE BRASS FLOOR-DRAIN IS OPEN, THE FLOOD WATERS ARE BEGINNING TO RECEDE!
BUT WHAT DO I DO WITH THESE SOGGY OLD COUPONS?
UHH... REDEEM 'EM?
GURGLE
AND SPEAKING OF REDEMPTION, WE'RE ALLOWING ALL OF YOU TO LEAVE IN PEACE!
LIKE ME, YOU'RE DANGEROUS! UNLIKE ME, YOU'VE GOT A CODE OF HONOR! YAY!
-DRIED
AGNA
SPINACH
WITHIN MINUTES, THE SUN RISES AND DANEBOE'S DAY BEGINS...
WELL, THAT'S THE LAST OF THE MOPPING...
Daneboe's
...ALL THAT'S LEFT FOR ME TO DO IS TO REPLACE THE STORE'S STOCK THAT SUSTAINED WATER-DAMAGE!
SO WATER YOU WAITIN' FOR, NERVILLE? GET CRACKIN', KID! HAHAHAHAHA-HAAA!
bleep bleep bleep
HELLO? OH, HI, MR. MANGELMANNER! YESSIR, WE-- ER, I TOOK CARE OF THE FLOOD!
YESSIR, I'M FINISHING THE CLEAN-UP RIGHT NOW! UHH, YOU WANT ME TO DO WHAT? WELL, YESSIR, IF YOU INSIST...
HEY, DID THE BOSS WANT YOU TO EVICT THAT "TRIBE OF LOST FOOD"?
NO, BUT HE ORDERED ME TO HOSE DOWN THE STORE'S ENTIRE PRODUCE SECTION! BUT NOW I'M SCARED THAT I MIGHT FLOOD THIS PLACE ALL OVER AGAIN!
END!

WATCH OUT FOR PAPERCUT<u>Z</u>™

Welcome to the spoilage-free second *ANNOYING ORANGE* graphic novel from **PAPERCUT<u>Z</u>**. We're the folks dedicated to publishing great graphic novels for all ages. I'm your annoying Editor-in-Chief, Jim Salicrup, here to—

HEY! HEY! JIM SAUERKRAUT!

Well, for Smurf's sake! Look who it is! That famously funny fruit and star of YouTube, Cartoon Network, and now Papercutz graphic novels-- ANNOYING ORANGE! Are you here to give us the inside poop on Dane Boedigheimer—

WHAT DID YOU SAY? THERE'S POOP INSIDE YOUR OFFICE?! *THAT'S DISGUSTING!* MAYBE YOU SHOULD CALL YOURSELVES POOPERCUTZ? HAHAHAHAHA!

Oh, Orange! I can never get enough of your clever witticisms! Surely you know that "inside poop" is a quaint fun phrase for "inside information"! And as I was saying, you probably have some insights on Dane Boedigheimer—

DANE BO-DING-DONG-HEIMER-WHAT?! THE ONLY DANEBO I KNOW IS THE SUPERMARKET I SPEND MOST OF MY TIME AT! MAYBE NERVILLE KNOWS WHO DANE BOE-DEE-OH-DOUGH IS, 'CAUSE I SURE DON'T! AND DON'T CALL ME "SHIRLEY."

Ha! There's that sophisticated wit of yours again! Well, even though you're pretending to be unaware of —

NOW YOU'RE TALKING ABOUT HIS "UNDERWEAR"? WHAT KINDA COMPANY IS POOPERCUTZ? I THOUGHT YOU GUYS DID STUFF FOR ALL-AGES? I'M NOT SURE IF YOU GUYS SHOULD BE DOING MY GRAPHIC NOVELS AFTER ALL – YOU MAY BE TOO GRAPHIC!

You silly punster! You know full well that Mike Kazaleh and Scott Shaw! the writer/artists who create your comics are also contributors to your Cartoon Network show—

WITH THOSE GUYS, YOU CAN START THE CARTOON NUTWORK! HAHAHAHA!

Be that as it may, we're almost out of room. I have just enough space left to tell everyone to keep an eye out for our next graphic novel, ANNOYING ORANGE #3 "Pulped Fiction"! Wow, I can't believe you let me finish that plug!

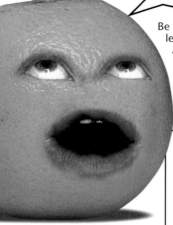

HEY, I'M ANNOYING, *NOT STUPID!*

STAY IN TOUCH!

EMAIL: salicrup@papercutz.com
WEB: www.papercutz.com
TWITTER: @papercutzgn
FACEBOOK: PAPERCUTZGRAPHICNOVELS
REGULAR MAIL: Papercutz, 160 Broadway, Suite 700, East Wing, New York, NY 10038

DANE BOEDIGHEIMER

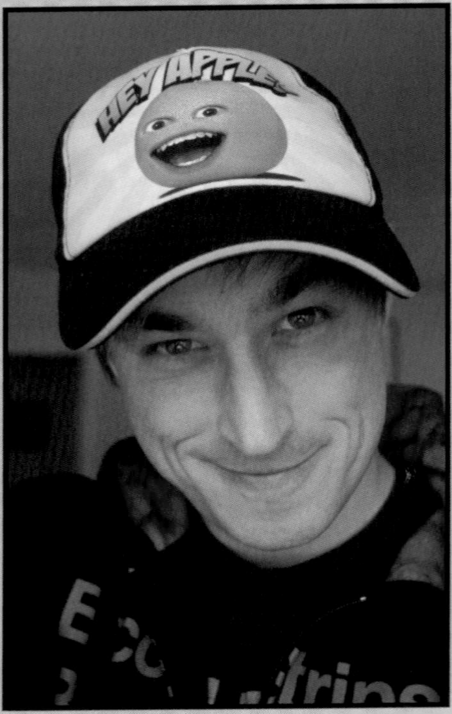
HEY APPLE!

Dane (or Daneboe as he's known online) is a filmmaker and goofball extraordinaire. Dane spent most of his life in the glamorous Midwest, Harwood, North Dakota, to be exact. With nothing better to do, (it was North Dakota) at around the age of twelve, Dane began making short movies and videos with his parents' camcorder. Since then he has made hundreds, if not thousands of short web videos… many of which are only funny to him. But Dane has remained determined to make "the perfect short comedy film;" one that will end all social problems and bring laughter to all the children of the world.

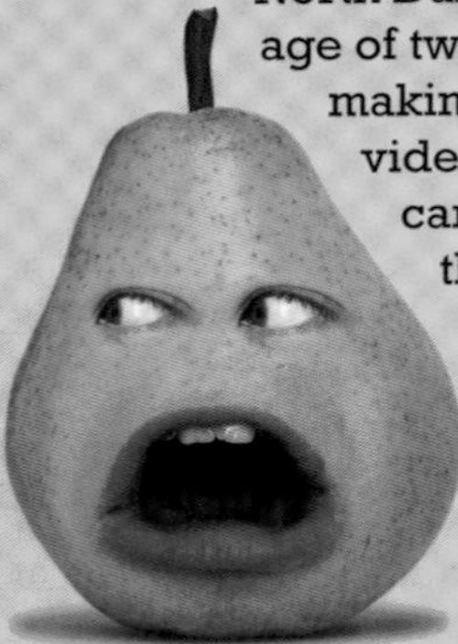

Currently, Dane is most widely known for creating The Annoying Orange, one of the most successful web series ever. The Annoying Orange has over 2 million subscribers and over 1 billion video views on YouTube as well as over 11 million facebook fans. On top of that, The Annoying Orange has a top rated show on Cartoon Network! As a result, fans have clamored for all sorts of cool Annoying Orange toys, t-shirts, games, etc. And despite all the wonderful stuff that has already appeared, fans still want more, and we suspect they'll be getting it.

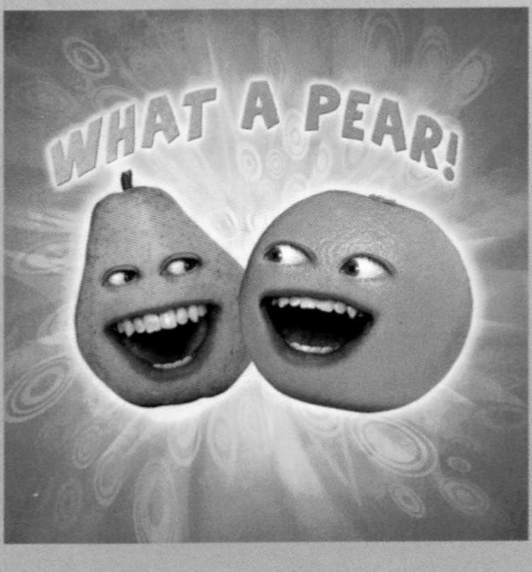
WHAT A PEAR!

Not to be completely undone, Dane's other videos have been viewed over 650 million times and have been featured on TV, as well as some of the most popular entertainment, news, and video sharing sites on the Internet.

In Dane's downtime he enjoys… oh, who are we kidding? Dane doesn't have any downtime. He wouldn't know what to do with himself if he did.

WATCH OUT FOR PAPERCUTZ™

Welcome to the spoilage-free second 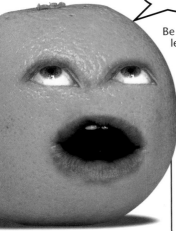 ANNOYING ORANGE graphic novel from **PAPERCUTZ**. We're the folks dedicated to publishing great graphic novels for all ages. I'm your annoying Editor-in-Chief, Jim Salicrup, here to—

HEY! HEY! JIM SAUERKRAUT!

Well, for Smurf's sake! Look who it is! That famously funny fruit and star of YouTube, Cartoon Network, and now Papercutz graphic novels-- ANNOYING ORANGE! Are you here to give us the inside poop on Dane Boedigheimer—

WHAT DID YOU SAY? THERE'S POOP INSIDE YOUR OFFICE?! *THAT'S DISGUSTING!* MAYBE YOU SHOULD CALL YOURSELVES POOPERCUTZ? HAHAHAHAHA!

Oh, Orange! I can never get enough of your clever witticisms! Surely you know that "inside poop" is a quaint fun phrase for "inside information"! And as I was saying, you probably have some insights on Dane Boedigheimer—

DANE BO-DING-DONG-HEIMER-WHAT?! THE ONLY DANEBO I KNOW IS THE SUPERMARKET I SPEND MOST OF MY TIME AT! MAYBE NERVILLE KNOWS WHO DANE BOE-DEE-OH-DOUGH IS, 'CAUSE I SURE DON'T! AND DON'T CALL ME "SHIRLEY."

Ha! There's that sophisticated wit of yours again! Well, even though you're pretending to be unaware of —

NOW YOU'RE TALKING ABOUT HIS "UNDERWEAR"? WHAT KINDA COMPANY IS POOPERCUTZ? I THOUGHT YOU GUYS DID STUFF FOR ALL-AGES? I'M NOT SURE IF YOU GUYS SHOULD BE DOING MY GRAPHIC NOVELS AFTER ALL - YOU MAY BE TOO GRAPHIC!

You silly punster! You know full well that Mike Kazaleh and Scott Shaw! the writer/artists who create your comics are also contributors to your Cartoon Network show—

WITH THOSE GUYS, YOU CAN START THE CARTOON NUTWORK! HAHAHAHA!

Be that as it may, we're almost out of room. I have just enough space left to tell everyone to keep an eye out for our next graphic novel, ANNOYING ORANGE #3 "Pulped Fiction"! Wow, I can't believe you let me finish that plug!

HEY, I'M ANNOYING, *NOT STUPID!*

STAY IN TOUCH!

EMAIL: salicrup@papercutz.com
WEB: www.papercutz.com
TWITTER: @papercutzgn
FACEBOOK: PAPERCUTZGRAPHICNOVELS
REGULAR MAIL: Papercutz, 160 Broadway, Suite 700, East Wing, New York, NY 10038

DANE BOEDIGHEIMER

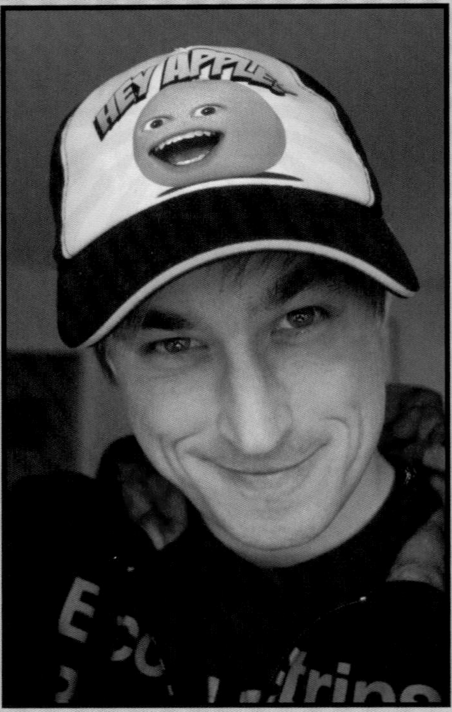

Dane (or Daneboe as he's known online) is a filmmaker and goofball extraordinaire. Dane spent most of his life in the glamorous Midwest, Harwood, North Dakota, to be exact. With nothing better to do, (it was North Dakota) at around the age of twelve, Dane began making short movies and videos with his parents' camcorder. Since then he has made hundreds, if not thousands of short web videos… many of which are only funny to him. But Dane has remained determined to make "the perfect short comedy film;" one that will end all social problems and bring laughter to all the children of the world.

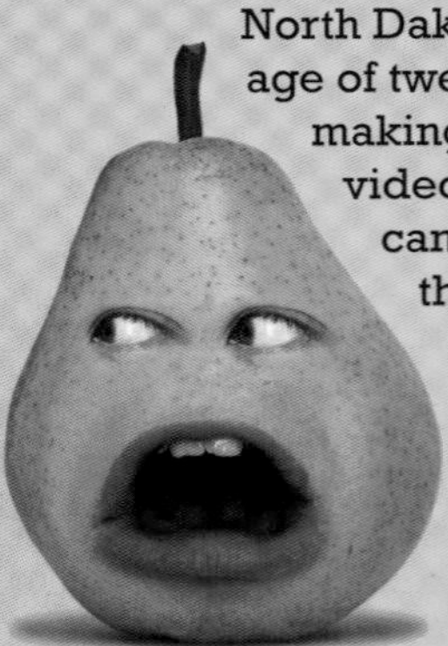

Currently, Dane is most widely known for creating The Annoying Orange, one of the most successful web series ever. The Annoying Orange has over 2 million subscribers and over 1 billion video views on YouTube as well as over 11 million facebook fans. On top of that, The Annoying Orange has a top rated show on Cartoon Network! As a result, fans have clamored for all sorts of cool Annoying Orange toys, t-shirts, games, etc. And despite all the wonderful stuff that has already appeared, fans still want more, and we suspect they'll be getting it.

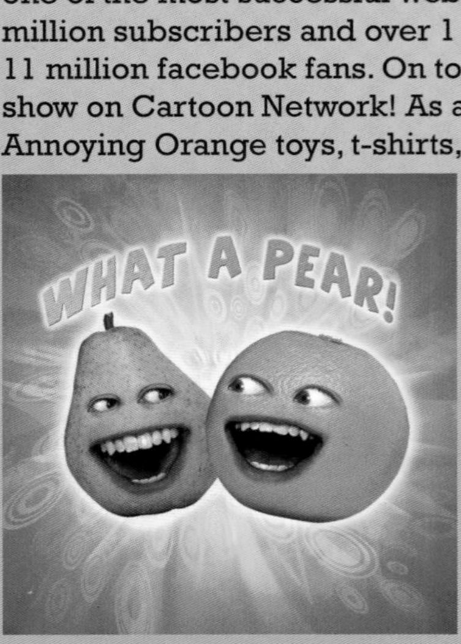
WHAT A PEAR!

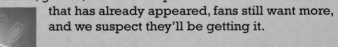

Not to be completely undone, Dane's other videos have been viewed over 650 million times and have been featured on TV, as well as some of the most popular entertainment, news, and video sharing sites on the Internet.

In Dane's downtime he enjoys… oh, who are we kidding? Dane doesn't have any downtime. He wouldn't know what to do with himself if he did.

SPENCER GROVE

Spencer Grove has written plays, prose, television scripts and more online videos than any sane person should attempt. Also, he bakes a mean apple pie.

He began his career in independent productions, working on everything from infomercials to award shows, eventually moving to MTV where he served as an Associate Producer on Pimp My Ride. Since 2009, he has served as the head writer of the Annoying Orange web series, creating and co-creating the supporting cast and developing the ever-expanding online world of the Orange.

Below: A title card illustrated by Mike Kazaleh.

ANNOYING ORANGE in:
"BOYS VS. GIRLS"

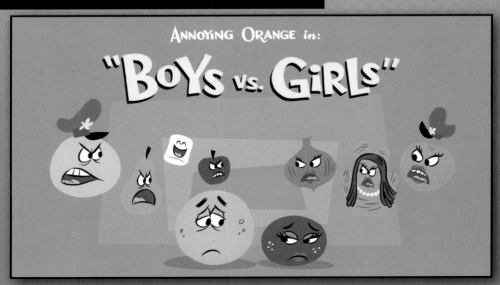

SCOTT SHAW!

Scott Shaw! is an example of Hunter S. Thompson's statement: "When the going gets weird, the weird turn pro." An award-winning cartoonist/writer of comicbooks, animation, advertising and toy design, Scott is also a historian of all forms of cartooning. After writing and drawing a number of underground "comix," Scott has worked on many mainstream comicbooks, including: SONIC THE HEDGEHOG (Archie); SIMPSONS COMICS, BART SIMPSON'S TREEHOUSE OF HORROR and RADIOACTIVE MAN (Bongo); WEIRD TALES OF THE RAMONES (Rhino); and his co-creation with Roy Thomas, CAPTAIN CARROT AND HIS AMAZING ZOO CREW! (DC). Scott has also worked on numerous animated cartoons, including: producing/directing of John Candy's Camp Candy (NBC/DIC/Saban) and Martin Short's The Completely Mental Misadventures of Ed Grimley (NBC/Hanna-Barbera Productions); Garfield and Friends (CBS/Film Roman); and the Emmy-winning Jim Henson's Muppet Babies (CBS/Marvel Productions).

Above: an example of Scott's storyboards for the ANNOYING ORANGE TV series

As Senior Art Director for the Ogilvy & Mather advertising agency, Scott worked on dozens of commercials for Post Pebbles cereals with the Flintstones. He also designed a line of Hanna-Barbera action figures for McFarlane Toys. Scott was one of the comic fans who organized the first San Diego Comic-Con, where he has become known for performing his hilarious ODDBALL COMICS slide show. shawcartoons.com. Scott is also a gag man and storyboard cartoonist on Cartoon Network's ANNOYING ORANGE program. His favorite fruit is forbidden.

MIKE KAZALEH

Mike Kazaleh is a veteran of comicbooks and animated cartoons. He began his career producing low budget commercials and sales films out of his tiny studio in Detroit, Michigan. Mike soon moved to Los Angeles, California and since then he has worked for most of the major cartoon studios and comicbook companies.

He has worked with such characters as The Flintstones, The Simpsons, Mighty Mouse, Krypto the Superdog, Ren and Stimpy, Cow and Chicken, and Bugs Bunny, as well as creating his own independent comics including THE ADVENTURES OF CAPTAIN JACK. Before all this stuff happened, Mike was a TV repairman.

Below: A title card designed by Mike Kazaleh.

ANNOYING ORANGE in:
"Fruitloose"

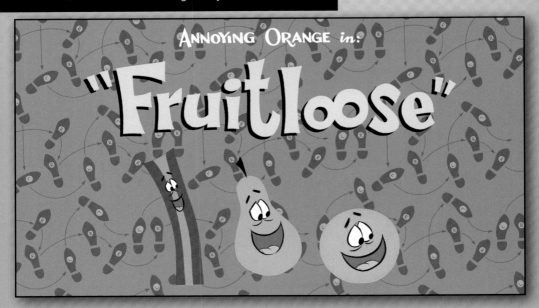